"I'm more than worth it. Let me prove it to you."

Christien uttered the daring words and deftly untied Tally's robe.

"I, uh—" The look in his eye and the way the material slid through his fingers stripped her of every chance of a witty comeback. The very idea of both silk and those rough and rugged hands caressing her skin at the same time left her speechless.

He pushed the robe off her shoulders and it floated to pool at her feet like liquid passion. "You look real good in red, Tally, but I'd bet you'd look even better in nothing, *cher*." His Cajun accent rang in her ears. His eyes were full of mischief.

"You don't play fair, Christien," she said, trying to regain her control. Something about his cocky smile stirred her tongue. She moved her hand to the belt of his jeans. Working the leather loose, unfastening the snap, she carefully lowered the zipper.

"You'll thank me later," he said.

Dear Reader,

After introducing Jack Castille's sexy brother Christien in the novella "Deliver Me," part of the *Red Letter Nights* anthology, I couldn't resist telling Tally and Christien's story. When I told my fellow anthology author Jeanie London my idea, she decided to join me, and so we've collaborated on the twins'—Tally and Bree—books. Both feature Gabriel Dampier, a sexy pirate ghost cursed by Belle Grand-mère for all eternity.

Our cursed pirate is tired of haunting Court du Chaud, and when he realizes that the twins are the key to breaking the evil spell governing his existence, he sets out to give them each a nudge into love. Come back with me to the coolest and the hottest place in the French Quarter and indulge yourself in Tally's journey, which leads her to ghosts, treasure and true love.

I hope you enjoy! I love to hear from my readers, so please drop me an e-mail at www.karenanders.com.

Karen Anders

Books by Karen Anders

HARLEQUIN BLAZE

GIVE ME FEVER
Karen Anders

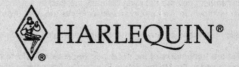

HARLEQUIN®

TORONTO • NEW YORK • LONDON
AMSTERDAM • PARIS • SYDNEY • HAMBURG
STOCKHOLM • ATHENS • TOKYO • MILAN • MADRID
PRAGUE • WARSAW • BUDAPEST • AUCKLAND

To Lyn and Darlene.
May all your dreams bring both of you
all the riches in the world.

ISBN 0-373-79223-9

GIVE ME FEVER

Prologue

THE MOON WAS OUT, full and yellow like a feral cat's eye. The wind blew gently, but it didn't touch him as he walked across the courtyard of Court du Chaud.

Court du Chaud would always be associated with his name, since he'd financed the building of the four rows of French colonial town houses that boxed in his very own mini-town within the city of New Orleans.

He passed the piazza where a woman's soft, sultry laughter sent his thoughts back to another moonlit night—a night full of drunken laughter and debauchery.

A mature, attractive woman flipped up her coat collar as he passed, the eerie sound of his boot heels echoing sadly.

He made his way up the stairs to the café where the pretty owner was closing up for the night. Taking one of the nearby chairs, he sat. She had a gorgeous aura, all pure-blue light, like the aching blue of a summer sky. She glowed with copper-rich, earthy power.

The man came out of the kitchen, the one whose aura used to be black with despair, like dark soot. It was now as pure blue as the café owner's, but pulsing with the golden light of a warrior, strong of heart, sure in battle.

"Stronger than you could ever be."

He turned to see his nemesis standing next to his chair. White hair, the color of bleached bones, lay thick and lank around her withered face. Her eyes, like dark wells of desolation, stared at him without emotion, except for the deep hatred that now seemed as much a part of her as the shawl that covered her stooped shoulders.

"I despise when you sneak up on me, Belle Grand-mère."

"It is for that very pleasure that I do it."

"There is not much more that can be done to me that has not already been done."

"You blackguard," she hissed. "Your suffering is like manna to me. I love to watch."

"You are a bloodthirsty, bitter old woman. Very bitter."

"And why shouldn't I be? My granddaughter lost everything, including her life. You never loved her, nor anyone or anything except gold and whoring."

He closed his eyes at the old woman's words, knowing in his heart that they had been true. But he wasn't that man anymore. Out of a dusty and dead past, the thought of young Madeline flowed with color and energy. He could see her, just as she'd been the moment he'd met her at the Celebration Ball.

Madeline had been draped in peach silk—a contrast to her ivory skin that would feel so very silky beneath his fingertips. Touch, a half-forgotten sense, bloomed to life.

For a fierce minute, he could almost taste her luscious lips, so real she was to him in the crucial silence. The sensation of her flowed over him and then was quickly gone. The ache that it brought remained.

"I may not have realized it until too late, but I loved Madeleine. Nothing you say or do will change that fact."

"You broke her heart and her spirit."

"And you punished me for it."

"Yes! You are doomed to walk the cobbles alone. I made certain of that in the voodoo curse I placed upon your soul. I also made certain your soul would remain here in Court du Chaud where you defiled my granddaughter, left her with twins in her belly and made her a pariah from society."

"But old woman, you tied your fate to mine."

She shrugged her thin shoulders. "Everything

comes with a price." She looked away and whispered, "Everything. I am sure my precious Madeleine discovered that too late."

"Her descendants—*our* descendants—have had to pay the most terrible price of all."

"You speak in riddles, pirate."

"You cursed our descendants with ambition, and forever robbed them of the chance for love." Even now, the words felt hollow and heavy on his soul.

"I *blessed* them so that they would not follow in Madeleine's footsteps and make fools of themselves in the name of love."

"Curses. Blessings. All a matter of opinion."

"I am connected to you through eternity." She sneered. "But since it is for revenge…it is worth it." Her voice echoed in his ears and then she disappeared.

Belle Grand-mère might derive great pleasure out of his pain, but he believed there was hope. He turned to look at the twins, Tallis and Breanne Addison, who had emerged from their respective townhomes.

He watched them walk toward the café. Their auras were lifeless pewter-gray, a gray heralding the sad fact that true love had never touched their beautiful souls.

These were the first twins born in their family in two hundred years. It might have signified a way to break the curse. The crone would never tell him outright, but he could speculate. He had watched his descendants for a very long time.

There must be a way to break the curse.

He turned his attention to the wall behind the counter. The full-length mural was painted with vibrant colors, depicting a pirate dressed in a rakish hat, a long plume of a feather stuck jauntily in the brim, his expression cocky and invulnerable.

The pirate's scarlet waistcoat with white piping and black velvet accents was meant to poke fun at the redcoats he and Jean Lafitte had defeated at the battle for New Orleans.

The pirate had also risked life and limb to smuggle in the folderols and trappings for the society of which he longed to be a part. What did he get for it? A boot in the face. Thumbing his nose at them, the pirate had built the elegant Court du Chaud—the "hot" court—right in their midst on prime property gifted to him by Lafitte.

But the tough, rakish man in the mural had learned nothing. Society would never accept him, not even after he had claimed an upper-class miss. Defiant and scorned, he'd sailed his flagship, *The Crescent,* to Texas to lick his wounds.

Off the coast of Texas, the pirate had finally found an enemy he could not fight.

Death.

He'd died looking up into the moonlit sky, the sounds of his breathing harsh, the noise of battle fading from his ears as his vision had dimmed.

Madeleine.

As his life had ebbed, he'd been given an epiphany. But cruel fate had robbed him of the chance to change, to make things right. His blood had seeped into the wooden deck and he had died with a curse upon his soul.

Gabriel Dampier gazed up at the image of himself, then out the window of the café to the twins below.

He'd been dead over two hundred years.

But was his salvation now upon him?

1

"TALLY, DO YOU HAVE a moment?"

Tally Addison turned at the sound of the man's voice. The owner of the Blue Note, where Tally sang four nights a week, stood in the doorway of her quasi-dressing room, looking more uncomfortable than usual. A tall, lanky man with a shock of carrot-red hair, Chuck Sommers was a kind, unassuming guy. Singing at the Blue Note was her passion, but didn't pay the bills. For that, she worked full-time for Chloe Matthews at Café Eros in Court du Chaud. "Hey, Chuck, sure."

Chuck came in and closed the door to the tiny room. He sat awkwardly on a stool close to Tally's dressing table. Even three days after Christmas, the Note was packed to capacity and Tally still had one set to sing.

"I'm selling the Blue Note," he said, his eyes shifting away from hers.

For a moment Tally couldn't believe what he was

saying. It was too early. She made an effort to keep the disappointment out of her voice. "I thought you said you'd be here for another three years."

"I know what I said, but my daughter is going through a divorce and she lives over in the Florida Panhandle. I'm going to open up a restaurant there and she's going to manage it for me. I know how much you love this place. I thought I'd give you first crack at it."

"What is your asking price?"

When he told her, she felt her heart sink. "I appreciate that, Chuck. How much time do I have?"

"I can give you two weeks, and then I'll have to put it on the market. I'm sure sorry, Tally."

She was devastated. She couldn't lose this place before she had the chance to realize her ambition. "It's not your fault, Chuck. Your daughter needs you and you have to do what's right for your family. I fully understand."

After Chuck left, Tally sat in front of her mirror for a long time. She did fully understand what Chuck was going through. Tally and her sister Bree had dropped everything to care for their brother when their mother had abandoned him at fourteen. Family always had to come first.

It didn't help that her plan of owning, managing and singing at a place like the Blue Note would never be realized if she couldn't come up with the cash to meet the asking price.

Unless she found Captain Gabriel Dampier's treasure.

Sure, she could work elsewhere then hopefully purchase some other club, but this opportunity had fallen into her lap—now.

She'd been searching estate sales, pawnshops, junk shops and antique stores for anything and everything that had to do with the captain. She'd found so much stuff, her attic was filled to the rafters, but, unfortunately, no treasure map.

As a direct descendent of the infamous pirate captain, Tally had firsthand knowledge that a treasure did exist. The information had been handed down through generations. For as long as Tally could remember, her mother had talked about Dampier's treasure and the pirate himself.

In fact, her uncle Guidry Addison had willed his Court du Chaud town house, the very house where Gabriel had lived, to her and Bree. She and her sister had renovated the large town house into a duplex with both girls living side by side and sharing a porch.

Before her uncle had died, he'd told her many tales about the treasure, the voodoo curse on the pirate and the fact that he haunted the court, trapped there for all eternity.

She had two short weeks to find the map or the Blue Note would go to someone else.

She wasn't about to let that happen.

TALLY SURVEYED her little compact car stuffed to the top with Captain Dampier paraphernalia that she'd just picked up at an estate sale. She'd found tons of books and journals in the old mansion's library that she wanted to go through along with a compass and spyglass reported to belong to the pirate.

In life, the captain had never been given his due. She hoped that she could rectify that by setting up a society and museum to showcase and honor him. If she ever found the treasure. If she ever managed to buy the Blue Note.

Late for her shift, she had no time to unload her car. She locked it and headed for the café.

Café Eros was located in a two-level town house at the mouth of the alley that served as the entrance to Court du Chaud. With an intimate atmosphere, it comfortably seated about thirty people with a decadent lounge at the top level and a café on the lower level that included outside seating situated around a small nonworking fountain full of bright flowers. The inside and outside tables were still decked out in red and green as the Christmas holiday had just passed.

The court itself was graced by a piazza, a large square of tumbled stones purportedly handcrafted and built by the notorious pirate Captain Gabriel Dampier. It sat in the middle of the court complete with park benches and greenery to give the tenants some measure of peace on a hectic day.

The huge Christmas tree was still situated in the center of the piazza and wouldn't be taken down until after New Year's Day. It was also the spot they shot off the spectacular fireworks display that was a tradition every year since Tally could remember.

She went upstairs to the kitchen and grabbed an apron and tied it around her waist. Picking up a pad and a pencil, she headed out to start her shift.

By scrimping and saving for a few years, she'd been singing at the Blue Note and had amassed a small amount of money. But she knew it would not be enough to buy the club and no bank was going to take a risk on a twenty-three-year-old waitress with no credit. She couldn't even mortgage the Court du Chaud property, since she and Bree had already done so to make the needed renovations.

Everything hinged on the treasure.

Through the open window of the café, Tally watched Jack Castille approach with Chloe on his arm. They were laughing, lost in each other. For a brief moment, Tally wondered what that feeling would be like, and then it faded.

Love was the watchword for the whole court, it seemed. Chloe and Jack weren't the only victims of the Court du Chaud love bug. Frequent patrons to Café Eros and residents of the court had also succumbed over Christmas.

The week after Christmas only seemed to strengthen love run rampant. Love. Ha. Tally didn't believe in fairy tales and happily-ever-after. She believed in cold hard cash and getting ahead. She didn't label her plans as dreams; she thought of them as goals. Dreams were elusive and insubstantial. Dreams were for suckers.

CLOSE TO THE END OF HER SHIFT, Tally walked into the kitchen where Chloe was busy making a dessert. Etta James's smoky vocals filtered through the café from the café's state-of-the-art sound system and hung in the air.

"Chloe, can I borrow Vincent at the end of my shift?" Vincent was the eighteen-year-old homeless boy Chloe had hired over Christmas. "I need his help in moving some boxes from my car to my town house."

"Sure," Chloe said. "He's delivering some croissants to Madame Alain right now."

"Great. Did Jack leave?" Tally asked, looking around the kitchen.

"Yes, he had errands to run."

"He spends so much time here you should put him to work," Tally said.

"Yeah, about as much time as Christien." Chloe gave Tally a sly look.

Tally shrugged. "Christien likes your gumbo."

"It's not my gumbo he comes here for, Tally, and you know it." Chloe drizzled caramel sauce over a slice of praline cheesecake.

"It won't do him any good. I'm not interested."

"Yeah, right," Chloe said, turning to look at her. "I may not be able to read minds, but I can read emotions and yours are pulsing a vibrant red right now."

"Okay." Tally threw up her hands. "He *is* hot. His accent is so smooth it curls my toes. And he's got the finest ass to ever fill out a pair of jeans—his brother should arrest him because it's so criminal. In fact, I want him to make me scream out his name. Satisfied?"

"Name the time and place, *chère.*"

Tally closed her eyes at Christien's soft, sexy voice. Opening them, she glared at Chloe, but she only looked at Tally with laughing eyes.

Chloe picked up a plate and breezed past her, forcing Tally to turn around and face Christien.

"I need to deliver this dessert," Chloe said.

"Chloe…"

"I'll be right back." Chloe flashed a wide-open perky smile. But her eyes glowed like one of Satan's helpers. She raised her brows a couple of times then exited the kitchen. That left Tally standing in the middle of the room, ogling the Cajun stud who was leaning against the door frame as if he owned the air-space.

The man made her feel hot and bothered just by existing. Whenever their eyes met from across the court or across the table, the smoldering heat she'd seen in them startled her.

She silently appreciated his lean, rock-solid physique and his confident, I-don't-give a-damn stance.

The red cotton T-shirt he wore clung to his broad shoulders and tapered to a flat stomach, and his well-worn jeans were snug in all the right places, accentuating narrow hips and hard, strong-looking thighs.

There was a rugged edge about him, just enough to give her the impression that he would be a major handful in anything he did.

She licked her lips and shoved her hands into her apron pockets. "I was talking about someone else," she blustered.

A quick grin formed on one of the most sensual-looking mouths she'd ever seen on a man.

"Do I look like I just came out of the bayou?"

No, he didn't. He looked delectable and irresistible, but she'd bite her tongue before she gave him any more ammunition. His gorgeous masculine features were backdropped by thick black hair pulled off his face and tied at his neck in a queue. He stepped forward and she felt her breathing deepen, felt her body warm…her skin tingle.

Sexual magnetism.

It was all there, clamoring inside her, making her move backward until she hit the kitchen counter.

He came to a direct stop in front of her, his thigh barely brushing her knees, making her completely aware of him, of his presence.

Very casually, he placed one hand on either side of her, boxing her in, his wide shoulders blocking her view of everything except him.

How could she protest when he smelled so amazingly good? This close, she could see that his irises were a beautiful, stunning shade of brown, shot with shards of deep gold and rimmed in black. His eyes seared straight to her soul.

Then his full lips curved into a disarming smile that made her melt inside. She held her breath, captivated by his gaze and that arresting grin of his as she waited for him to speak.

"You can deny it to yourself, Tally, and you can even deny it to all your friends, but I know what I see when I look at you," he whispered, his voice a deep, delicious baritone. "I feel it when you're near."

She hardened her resolve. She would not be intimidated by this man. "What's that?"

"Sex. It vibrates around you as if your body is already affected by mine and I haven't even touched you."

Desire took hold, coiling low and deep inside her. She ached to touch him, feel his skin beneath her palm. With that thought, the floodgates opened and everything she had thought in private poured free.

Temptation.

It felt so good, so thrilling and exciting and forbidden; she wanted to drown in the sensation.

But now, with Christien standing in front of her looking one-hundred-percent virile, she wanted to let go for the first time in a long time.

His gaze darkened, making her nipples pucker tight in response. "It must be nice to be so cocky," she said.

He lifted his hand and gently smoothed his fingers down the side of her neck. She watched, mesmerized, as he slowly dipped his head toward hers, and her heart thumped erratically in her chest. At first, she thought he was going to kiss her, but he bypassed her parted lips and grazed his jaw along hers, until his mouth came to rest against the shell of her ear.

She heard him inhale deeply, filling his lungs with the scent of her skin and hair before releasing it in a long, slow exhale and murmuring into her ear, "It is in more ways than one, *chère*."

He pulled away from her to look deep into her eyes. "I'm a patient man. But don't keep me waiting too long."

"What exactly are you doing here?"

"I came for a bowl of gumbo, just like you said. But I can be persuaded to go to work for you…you don't need a kid to move those boxes. You need a man."

TALLY WAS FANNING HERSELF when Chloe returned to the kitchen.

Chloe shook her head. "You might as well give in, Tally. If he's anything like Jack, you're a goner."

"Chloe, I wish you would stop trying to matchmake us. Just because the whole court has gone crazy over one another, doesn't mean I'm going to succumb." Tally pulled a bowl out of the cupboard.

"You won't be able to resist."

"Are you getting a vibe or just being a smarty-pants?" She dished up some of Chloe's delicious gumbo.

Chloe gave Tally a little smile and a shrug. "Being a smarty-pants. Why are you so determined to over-look a really good man?"

"I'm determined to rely on myself, Chloe. It's safer that way."

Chloe put her hands on her hips. "You're going to find out, Tally, that sometimes you have to rely on other people."

"I hope not. When I find Captain Dampier's trea-sure, I'll be able to call all the shots."

"That old story again. Tally, there's no treasure. Your old uncle Guidry was very eccentric."

"You mean crazy. No, he wasn't and neither is my mother."

Chloe shook her head. "You might as well be chasing your uncle's ghost."

"Scoff all you want, but I'm going to find that loot."

Tally grabbed a beer out of the fridge and headed for the door. Chloe put her hand on her arm and said, "Just give him a chance. He might surprise you."

Tally smiled, but it didn't have anything to do with amusement. "I don't like surprises. I don't need a man like that twisting me up inside and making me lose my focus. I'd rather pursue my own ambitions. I know who I can count on. Me."

"You can't curl up with a treasure chest at night. Ambition is nice and all but…love is wonderful."

"I'm sure it is…for you and Jack, but like I told you before, I'm not like you. Now that my brother Mark's all grown up, it's time to get what *I* want."

"If you're really finished mothering Mark, why do you worry about him so much?"

Tally didn't know how to respond. Chloe was right of course.

"You'd better go deliver that gumbo, before Christien comes back here wondering where it is," suggested Chloe.

Tally rolled her eyes. "Exactly. And I'd better get back to work. My boss is a real slave driver."

Chloe's laughter followed Tally out of the kitchen. Tally was very happy for Chloe, who seemed much more lighthearted and less overworked these days. She'd finally relinquished some of the everyday duties and had actually taken a weekend off since she'd hired Vincent.

As she approached the table, the sight of Christien twisted her insides with want. Setting down the bowl of gumbo, she said, "Is there anything else I can get you?"

"Yes, Tally, but I'll wait until you're ready to give it to me."

Her eyes drifted down to that delectable mouth.

"You're insufferable." But she couldn't help the smile that played on her lips.

"I have a feeling that you like that about me."

"Enjoy the gumbo."

His fingers slid seductively around her wrist before she could turn away. "Have dinner with me tomorrow night."

"No." The feel of his fingers on her skin made her nerves go haywire. Should she give in to her lust for this man? Where would it lead?

"Tally, you're breaking my heart."

She walked away, muttering under her breath, "Better yours than mine."

Captain Gabriel Dampier stood beneath his mural watching the crone who hovered right beside Christien's table. It was fascinating to see how intent she was. She looked almost…worried.

Maybe Belle Grand-mère found Castille a threat to her curse. Castille and Tally did spark off each other. It was like watching a rainbow ripple and dance whenever the two of them came close to each other.

He watched as Tally rebuffed Christien once more. The chit was a handful and stubborn, just like Madeleine.

He hadn't felt human flesh in two hundred years,

but he'd never forget how his Madeline had felt against him, beneath him.

He'd witnessed the encounter in the kitchen and Gabriel had been so sure that the chit would give in.

He'd also overheard in the kitchen that she was looking for his treasure. He smiled, thinking about how people had been looking for his hoard for years.

That old man—what was his name?—was always yelling about treasure and Gabriel Dampier's ghost. Guidry. Right. But everyone just thought he was a lunatic. Gabriel had been content to take that secret to the grave, but now he wondered if maybe revealing the whereabouts of the treasure might work to his advantage.

She would need help. Perhaps Christien Castille could be of service? He was a man as worthy as Lafitte.

This time it would be Gabriel's turn to torture the old woman. "You look worried, Belle Grand-mère."

She turned her eyes away from Christien. "He's trouble. Reminds me of you."

He peered at her, realization dawning. "He's the catalyst, is he not?"

She twisted the edges of her shawl. "What are you prattling about? He will not coerce her into love. I blessed my descendents with enough ambition to spurn love."

"And if he does coerce her?"

"He will fail."

"It will break this curse, crone, will it not? I will be free at last."

"You will fail, Gabriel, as you have failed in everything, lost everything. You'll spend eternity paying for what you did to my granddaughter."

"I did not understand at the time that my love would destroy her. I regret it down to the deepest part of my soul. Is that not enough?" he snarled.

Her lips pinched and her eyes narrowed, hatred gleamed there and had only strengthened over the centuries they'd been locked together. "No. It will never be enough."

He studied Christien himself. "What will happen if the girl gives up her ambition for love?"

The old woman had no answer to that.

"It will break the curse," Gabriel said.

"Only half of the curse," she agreed with reluctance. "Another concession I had to make for the voodoo I used is the possibility for you to redeem yourself."

"How?"

The crone eyed him.

He made a noise of disgust and spat, "You were never a fair woman."

Belle Grand-mère's eyes flashed and she snarled again, "More fair than you, blackguard."

"Give me a fighting chance."

She looked away and said, "You can materialize to the girl to aid you in your bid for salvation."

"Your revenge has been cruel. To make me wait for two hundred years without hope. Why?"

"For the enjoyment. I do not care a whit about you."

"You should examine what it means to forgive, old woman, lest you be lost forever."

She sniffed and scowled, ignoring his words. "Take heed, Gabriel. You must get both girls to give up their ambitions for love. Nothing less will break the curse. But let me warn you. If you fail, you'll have to wait two hundred years for another chance."

2

TALLY STOOD IN THE DOORWAY of the spare room in her town house where she did research in her attempt to find Dampier's treasure. She had a desk and computer and an intricate filing system for clues. Christien's biceps bulged as he set down the last box.

She'd had to eat crow and graciously accept Christien's help, since Vincent hadn't returned by the end of Tally's shift.

Christien trailed after her as she led him back downstairs. After she opened the front door, Tally turned to him. Her breath caught in her throat at the way his hot eyes bore into hers. She stared at him, enthralled by the way the sun shone on his hair and highlighted that mouth. The mouth she wanted to press against hard and explore with her tongue.

Slowly stepping toward her, he backed her into the shadowed foyer and up against the nearest wall, bracing his hands on either side of her shoulders.

Trapped in the vee of his arms, her gaze locked brazenly with his. Seconds passed, filling the air between them with subtle expectation and deeper desires.

Tally slipped her fingers into the belt loops on his soft jeans. She pulled him closer until their bellies, hips, and thighs were intimately aligned and his thickening shaft found a welcoming home at the notch between her legs.

A blissful sigh escaped her, and she whispered, "I've been wondering something, Christien. I've been wondering if you'd taste as dark and decadent as you look."

"This from a woman who wouldn't have dinner with me," he murmured.

"Dinner is personal. Sex, as we both know, can be very casual."

Singed to the core by her admission and inflamed by a man she'd fantasized about for a month, she reached up and pulled the band from his queue, threading her fingers through the silky strands around his handsome face. She cupped the back of his neck and pulled his mouth down to her waiting lips tingling with anticipation.

Unable to take it slow, her devouring mouth pressed hard against his. Her tongue swept into his mouth and tangled with his and she tasted the pure, unadulterated sensuality that was so much a part of him. She shivered, unable to stop the sultry ache spreading through her belly, or the slick moisture settling between her thighs.

She felt a low growl rumble up from his chest. He palmed the back of her head to hold her in place and slanted his mouth across hers, taking control of the kiss.

Her breasts swelled within the confines of her dress, and she shifted restlessly against him, wanton and needy as his lips and tongue continued their lush, hungry assault on her mouth and senses.

She knew what she was getting herself into here and part of her was concerned about the future. Her relationships had always been impossible.

With that thought filling her mind though her body was desperate for more, her hands went to his belt.

A crash startled them apart. Across the room, Tally's entertainment center had overturned, smashing her TV and CD player into rubble.

Bree's door flew open and she shouted, "Tally, what the hell…"

Bree's eyes widened at Christien. "Who are you?"

"It's okay, Bree. It's Christien, Jack's brother."

"Oh, I didn't recognize you for a minute. Why are you standing like… Right. My brain must be fried."

All of a sudden Tally came to her senses. "Christien was just leaving," she said. Whispers of her lack of judgment flooded her ears.

His dark, seductive eyes that promised they had more to discuss between them held Tally's gaze until she turned away to talk to Bree, who entered the living room.

Bree saw the mess and murmured, "Oh my, what happened?"

"When we meet again, *chère,* I'll show you how good I can be." With a wide grin, Christien left.

Tally closed the door.

"I don't know, Bree. It just fell."

"I'll get a broom," Bree offered. "Jeez, Tally, I'm so sorry. He was kissing you, huh?"

"Yes, Bree. But I was the one who started it."

Her sister stood there for a moment and then said, "Damn, he's hot."

Tally and Bree were as rock solid as sisters could be. Twins shared a special bond and it was certainly there between the two of them. Bree was younger by five minutes.

At eighteen they had banded together to take care of their fourteen-year-old brother when their mother had deserted them all. Most people would think that would have been a destabilizing event in their lives, but surprisingly, it had been one of the best things their mother could have done. She had always been in debt, always searching for the quick fix and the fast buck.

Tally folded her arms across her chest. Her fingers tingling from the softness of Christien's hair.

She'd almost had sex with Christien right in her foyer and she marveled at the fact that she wished she was upstairs in her bedroom right now touching all that hot, gorgeous skin.

Sometimes getting saved by the bell wasn't all that it was cracked up to be.

"WILL YOU NEVER STOP plaguing me, you old crone!" Gabriel stood next to the overturned cabinet. He wished for one moment he could be solid enough to curl his fingers into satisfying fists, reach out his hands and throttle the old witch. Two hundred years of frustration poured through him. Two hundred years without peace, without forgiveness. Two hundred years of remorse eating at his soul.

"Did you think I was going to make it easy for you?" She smirked. "You wanted everything to be easy, didn't you? The golden boy of New Orleans," she scoffed. "But the one thing you wanted eluded you, so you used my granddaughter as your portal into the world you couldn't enter. A means to an end. Surprise, Gabriel. Redemption is not easy. I look at this as one more way to torment you. You'll never get

Tally to change her way of thinking. She's on her course and once she finds the map, your plan turns to dust."

"That's what you want, isn't it? You want Tally to have the treasure."

"Of course, I do. She deserves it." She moved closer to him, her wizened face taut with hatred. "Dust, Gabriel, just like your physical body. Dead and buried." She turned on her heel and walked through the wall.

Impotent rage slammed into him like a hurricane. He raised his boot heel right above the floorboard that hid what he wanted Tally to find. He slammed it down. Unexpectedly his foot had substance and the board cracked under the force. Both girls turned to look at the noise.

"What was that?" Bree asked.

"I don't know, but I'm getting goose bumps." Tally moved closer to the edge of the fallen entertainment center and peered into the lengthening shadows from the waning daylight. For a split second, she could swear that a ghostly shape of a man stood there, but he was no ordinary guy.

This man was dressed in what looked like a waistcoat and pantaloons. Unease prickled along her skin. As she moved closer she could smell candle wax and rosewater along with the overpowering smell of evergreen. She walked around the grand piano and turned on a corner lamp. Light flooded the area and cold flowed over her as Tally felt a presence.

"Did you see that?"

"What?" Bree asked, coming over to investigate.

"A ghost, I think?"

Bree looked at Tally, amusement dancing in her eyes. "The captain?"

Tally didn't smile back as she searched the area. When she saw the broken floorboard, she cried, "Dammit!" and knelt down, surveying the damage. "These floorboards are ancient. How am I going to repair this?"

"Easy," Bree said, "New Orleans is full of renovated houses with cypress floorboards. You'll have to do some trash-picking."

"Good idea." Shaken by the sight of the apparition she was almost certain was the ghost of Captain Dampier, Tally sidled away from the ruined floorboard back toward the grand piano as the hair on the back of her neck sprang to attention.

Had *he* turned over the entertainment center? Was he angry? Now that she'd seen him once, would he appear again? Would she have to constantly be on the look out for him?

She couldn't worry about this now. She had more pressing issues, like almost losing herself in Christien Castille, a real, live male.

"Thankfully it missed the baby grand," Tally said, rubbing at the glossy finish of the keyboard cover, her chill fading.

Bree agreed, then gave her sister a sly glance. "So, what's with the hunky Cajun?"

So much for subtlety. "It was a weak moment."

"Come on, Tally, from what you've told me about Christien, I don't know how you've resisted this long."

"Bree, I'm not interested in a *relationship*. You know that. The Blue Note's up for sale. I have to focus my energy on getting enough money to buy it."

"I thought the owner wasn't selling for a few years. How are you going to come up with the money to buy it now?"

"I'm going to find Dampier's treasure."

"Oh, Tally, Mom thought she could find it, too."

"Are you comparing me to Mom?"

"No, I just don't want you to get your hopes up too high. She was obsessed with finding the treasure and it came to nothing."

"I'll find the treasure, Bree. I'm not giving up the Blue Note and I know I won't have time for a relationship. Relationships never amount to much in our family. Look at Mom, she had many and for all we know is still alone."

"I'm not one to disagree, Tally. Look what happened with me and Jude."

"That creep tried to alienate you from all your friends including your family. He made a mistake when he tried to come between us."

"Yes, he did. No one can break our bond."

Tally and Bree were one in their philosophy about ambition. Work hard and do whatever it takes. Tally had the Blue Note in her sights and Bree was steadily working her way up to bigger and better things.

"Well, since a relationship is out of the question, why don't you just have hot, sweaty Cajun sex with him?" Bree said with a wry grin.

Tally laughed in spite of herself. "Cajun sex. That's a good one. You have such a way with words."

"Hey, I call 'em like I see 'em. He's too yummy to contemplate anything else."

"I'm not exactly ruling that out."

TWO DAYS LATER on Wednesday night, Tally reached over and grabbed her oven mitts, bending down to retrieve the hot, fragrant brownies out of the oven. As she turned, she promptly dropped the pan on the floor.

This time there was no mistaking the man she saw standing at the entrance to her living room, his arm outstretched, his finger pointing. His mouth moved, but Tally couldn't hear what he said.

Captain Gabriel Dampier.

Or more accurately, his ghost.

She started to walk toward him to get a better view and make sure she wasn't seeing things, when her bare toes hit the side of the brownie pan. Yelping at the pain, she looked down. Realizing the hot pan could do more damage to her old cypress floor, she quickly bent down to pick up the pan. When she straightened, the captain was gone.

Blinking her eyes several times, Tally peered at the spot where he'd just been. She set the pan down on the hot plate on the counter and walked toward the living room. If she were to follow that ghostly arm, she would end up right at her broken floorboard. What was he trying to tell her?

She went to the spot and turned on the floor lamp, but everything seemed ordinary. Bending down, she pulled at the loose board, pushing away pieces of broken wood. She could see nothing in the cavity and she certainly wasn't going to put her hand down there. Jumping up, she returned to her kitchen and opened her junk drawer, grabbing a flashlight.

Returning to the broken floorboard, she shone the light inside and gasped. The light reflected off intricately carved, well-worn wood. Her heart pounded. Reaching down, she pulled out a wooden box. An audible pop sounded when Tally gently lifted off the lid. As the pungent odor of ancient cedar drifted on the air, Tally looked inside, her breath trapped in her lungs. Nestled inside was a leather-bound book and a very old key. Very gently Tally picked up the volume, her hands shaking. Carefully she opened the cover and saw in beautiful spidery writing:

Captain Gabriel Dampier
Privateer and Rescuer of New Orleans
In his own words

It was the captain's journal. The ghost had wanted her to find it. She rose and walked to her dining-room table and sat down in one of the chairs. Turning to the first page she started to read:

It was at the Grand Celebration and Ball after our victory in battle that I first saw her— Madeleine.

The flag that hung over the ballroom proclaimed in bold letters JACKSON AND VICTORY! THEY ARE BUT ONE! Jackson himself was dancing with his sweet wife, Rachel, to the popular tune "Possum Up a Gum Tree." My friend and comrade, the king of the corsairs, Jean Lafitte, laughing and conversing with Governor Claiborne, trying to outdo each other with stories of the warrants they had issued on each other's head.

But amid all the frivolity and partying nothing else could draw my attention like that beautiful lady. She was a vision in a dress that seemed to float around her like the gossamer wings of a butterfly. I was smitten by the sight of her dark eyes and hair and had to have an introduction....

The sound of Tally's door banging open and her brother Mark's voice calling, "Honey, I'm home," forced her to slam the journal closed and rise with it in her hand.

"Hey, I smell brownies," he said, coming into her kitchen.

She dropped the journal on the counter to slap his hand as he reached for the pan. "Those are for my krewe meeting tonight."

"You doing krewe for Mardi Gras? Spare a few for your baby brother."

Tally perused her brother. *Baby* certainly did not fit him anymore. When had her brother gotten so...big? He was six feet tall and looked as solid as steel.

His thick, glossy brown hair needed a trim. The dark stubble on his face did nothing to detract from his tough appearance. She was sure women sighed when he walked by. It was hard to believe he'd grown from that young boy into this handsome man.

"There are fresh chocolate-chip cookies in the cookie jar. How about ice-cold milk to wash it down?" she said, shouldering his bulk out of the way and reaching for a glass.

"Stellar." He grinned, took the cookies, walked around to the stools she'd placed on the living-room side of the counter and sat.

"To what do I owe this visit?" She poured the milk and handed him the glass.

"Thought I'd stop by and say hey. I know how you get when I don't keep in touch."

"It worries me, Mark. How hard is it to give me a call once in a while?"

"You're always so intense. I'm nineteen, a grown-up."

"At nineteen you should be in your second year of college. Instead, you follow bands around toting equipment, setting it up, taking it down. You're better than that, Mark." Tally sighed.

"And you're better than a waitress, Tally."

"I know that, but Bree and I couldn't afford college, but we could help to send you now, Mark."

"And you never let me forget that you had to give up college."

"You know I would have given up more than college for you. But don't let it be in vain. We just want more for you."

He rolled his eyes, but Tally saw the anger there as well. "I like what I do."

"You can play any instrument known to man. You're wasting your time following bands around. You even write music—it's good. You could go to college, and then teach, compose, anything. You could be someone."

"I am someone." He set the half-eaten cookie down on the counter so hard it crumbled. "This is why I don't come over here."

His cell phone rang and Tally looked at the clock. Startled at the time, she said, "I have to go get ready for my meeting. Don't touch those brownies."

He nodded curtly, his eyes barely meeting hers. She suspected her nagging was driving her brother away, but why couldn't he work as hard as his sisters did? Have the same ambition as his sisters?

While she was upstairs changing her clothes, she heard her brother yell, "Tally, I need something to write on."

She was about to tell him there was a notepad in the junk drawer when he yelled out, "Never mind. Found something."

She had just finished brushing her hair when he called out again. "Hey, I've got to go. See ya later, sis. Thanks for the cookies."

He always seemed to appear and disappear at the most inopportune moments.

A short while later, she returned downstairs. At least her brownies were still there. Her eyes fell to the captain's journal lying open on the counter. The last page had almost been totally torn from the priceless journal. Furious that her brother had been so thoughtless as to use that for paper, she turned the torn page over. At the top of the remaining scrap in neat handwriting read, "A Map To My Treasure."

FIVE DAYS LATER on January fourth, she was still trying to find him. After long shifts at Café Eros, singing before a sold-out New Year's Eve crowd at the Blue Note, and her everyday chores, the time had flown by. She pulled her cell phone out of her pocket and dialed his number again. Mark had disappeared in the past, but he'd at least given her a call within a couple of days.

Okay, maybe she was overreacting. Mark was probably mad at her for saying those things about his precious roadie job. Entering her town house, she sat down in the living room, pulled her cell phone out of her pocket and dialed again.

Still no answer.

"Where are you?" she said.

She would need help. Christien. His name popped into her mind unbidden. A calming sensation flowed through her at just the thought of confiding in Christien Castille. He was a P.I. now and a former cop. He would help her if she asked.

And if Mark was in trouble, she'd never forgive herself if she didn't do something proactive.

She also needed the part of the map Mark had to find the treasure and buy the Blue Note. She didn't have much time left.

But ask Christien for help? It went against everything inside her. All her life she'd been determined to be independent and never lean on anyone too hard, even her sister, but Mark was her baby brother and she quite literally had no other choice. She wouldn't know the first thing about tracking someone down.

Waffling between worry and anger, Tally would burn her brother's inconsiderate ears when she got her hands on him.

She picked up her cell phone again and dialed Chloe's number. When she answered, Tally said, "Do you have Christien's work address?"

3

BEFORE HE WENT TO WORK on Monday, four days into the new year, Christien knelt down in front of the mausoleum and set the chrysanthemums down. He'd visited his mother's grave often over the years, but he never missed putting her favorite flowers on her grave on the anniversary of her death.

He'd quit the force six months ago when he'd lost it and punched a suspect in open court.

He remembered the day vividly. After the not-guilty verdict, the victim's daughter, Sarah Richardson had come up to him to tell him how much she'd appreciated everything he'd done to find the man who had robbed and murdered her mother. He'd thought he'd been right to immediately go to the suspect's home the moment they had arrested him on suspicion of his involvement in the case. The suspect's wife had given Christien and his partner permission to search the man's workshop where they'd found items that had belonged to Sarah's mother.

The defense attorney had argued that his client had reasonable expectation of privacy in his workshop, a place his wife never went. Therefore, the evidence that Christien had found had been suppressed. Even with Christien's testimony, they'd lost the case.

It was then that the suspect had walked past him with a smug look on his face, gloating about having beaten the system. Christien had snapped.

The victim's daughter had later told him that he'd at least given her closure by having the chance to look at the face of the man who had killed her mother.

Closure. It was something he had never achieved over his own mother's murder. He didn't have to be a shrink to understand the reason. Her killer had never been punished and that was also his fault.

Guilt swirled inside him as he gazed down at his mother's grave. His jaw tight, he slipped his hands into his jean pockets.

He'd only been six when he'd gotten up because he'd heard noises downstairs. He'd been home alone with his mother and had seen a man struggling with her, pushing her down. Her head hit the corner of the coffee table, fracturing her skull.

When it had come time for him to view the suspects collared in the murder, Christien hadn't been able to pick the man out of the lineup and his mother's killer had gotten away free.

His mother had been the stabilizing force in his family. He loved his father, but Christien identified with his mother. It had been twenty years since her death and, even though she was gone, he felt compelled to live up to the standards she'd set just by the way she'd lived her life.

He stood there for another few minutes and then turned away.

He'd have to admit to himself that P.I. work wasn't as fulfilling as being a cop.

Heading out of the cemetery to his Jeep, he drove over to his small office on the second floor of an eighteenth-century house that also served as the place of business for an antique store and an art gallery.

He climbed the stairs, stopping when he saw the flirty pink hem of a skirt. The skirt swished as the woman moved and she came into full view at the top of the stairs.

Tally Addison with her tight little backside and her uptight personality was actually standing in front of his office door.

Her gorgeous hair had been carelessly twisted into a mass of haphazard strands on top of her head and her matching eyes were a creamy, rich brown, almond shaped and exotic.

She looked incredibly sexy. He'd only seen her in her work clothes of jeans, T-shirt, and an apron that tied around her waist. Nothing overtly suggestive or clingy, but he'd seen enough of her coming and going to know that she had the kind of full, luscious figure he liked on a woman.

The simple green jersey-knit top she wore cupped her breasts and the curve of her slim waist, and the pink skirt gave him a tantalizing view of long slim legs.

She had soft, full lips and a sweet mouth designed to give a man all kinds of erotic pleasure. The thought caused his stomach to tighten with awareness.

But even with those centerfold curves and breathtaking beauty, what he liked most about Tally was her you-can't-intimidate-me attitude. Her independent nature was like a badge of courage and she wore it like armor.

He loved pushing her buttons. It was so easy. Her words in the kitchen of Café Eros reverberated through him.

I want him to make me scream out his name.

The woman made him feel like he was constantly running a fever through his blood, thick and hot—except this heat was pure sexual hunger, a craving for Tally in the most elemental, intimate way possible.

He was tormenting himself with these carnal thoughts, but that was nothing new. He'd been in physical agony ever since he'd met Café Eros's sexiest waitress.

Shaking off his surprise at Tally's impromptu visit, along with the thrum of arousal vibrating within him, he climbed the rest of the stairs to the landing.

"I hope you don't mind me just showing up."

"No, not at all." He opened his office door and settled his hand against her lower back as he ushered her inside, through the outer office and into his.

He indicated a chair and she sat down.

"So, you're here because…?"

She inhaled a deep breath, causing her breasts to rise and fall in a very beguiling way. "I need your services."

Her tone was very businesslike, but he couldn't stop the slow, shameless grin her double-edged words evoked. "Do you?"

Her eyes crackled at his blatant innuendo. "Your professional services. Since you're a private investigator, I was hoping I could hire you. My brother is missing."

Her statement took him momentarily off guard. While he'd been surprised that she'd shown up at his office, the last thing he'd expected was her needing this sort of help. Years of police training told him she was being completely straightforward and serious with her request, and the distress he detected in the depths of her eyes was real.

Feeling the first spark of interest since he'd left the force, his mind leaped to thoughts of an investigation. "Why don't you tell me what you know about your brother's disappearance from the beginning, and we'll go from there."

"I saw him on Wednesday night, but haven't been able to reach him since."

"So he's been missing for five days?"

"That's right."

"How old is your brother?"

"Nineteen."

"Where does he work?"

"All over the place. He works crew for a band."

"What band?"

"I don't think he works for any one band and I'm not really sure which bands. I didn't approve of his job and we didn't talk much about what he actually does."

"Has he done this in the past?"

"Well, yes, over the past year there have been times when he's been gone a day or two, but he's never been away this long without letting me know where he is."

"Have you reported this to the police?"

"I've filled out a missing person's report, but because of the nature of his job the police aren't treating it as a priority. My brother also has a habit of disappearing and not contacting me."

His gaze lingered on her profile. He was aware that the police couldn't dedicate a large number of resources to track down each and every missing person without signs of a crime.

"You do realize that he could be partying, gone off with friends, or maybe a girlfriend?"

"Yes, I do realize those things, but it's not like him to do this."

"I'll help you with this, Tally, but as a friend," he said, realizing he made the offer for more reasons than just to find her brother.

Spending time with Tally was a huge incentive, but Christien had a brother and a sister of his own, so he understood her worries. Besides, if he sent her home with platitudes, it would bother his conscience. Based on what Tally had told him about her brother, his gut told him he wasn't in mortal danger, but he'd never play Russian roulette with another person's life.

"I can pay you."

"But you don't have to."

She lifted her chin and squared her shoulders, and damned if he didn't detect a hint of vulnerability beneath all that bravado. "I insist. I don't need charity from you Christien. I'd rather pay my way."

"Suit yourself. I'll need as much information as you can give me on your brother." He withdrew an application from a side drawer for her to fill out. "Any bank-account numbers you know of, statements, credit cards, social-security number, driver's license. And I'll need a recent photograph of him, too. Give me anything you think would be helpful in tracing him."

"So how much do you usually charge for this kind of work?"

He named a price.

She winced. "How long do you think it'll take you to find him?"

"I don't know. For all we know, he could turn up tomorrow."

"I could only hope. I really want to find him as quickly as possible."

"I'll tell you what. Why don't we give it a week? After a week, I'll start charging you."

Her lips thinned into a determined line. "Sounds suspiciously like charity, Christien. I don't like to be indebted to anyone."

"You'd be doing me a favor. Ever since I left the force, I've been going crazy with the jobs I've been getting. The money is good, but I'm afraid they're not much of a challenge."

"I insist on paying you your normal retainer." She pulled out her checkbook and wrote an amount.

Christien moved away from the desk and squatted down in front of her chair. "You are a stubborn woman, but being the contrary guy that I am, I happen to like it."

He didn't take the check when she offered it to him, so she was forced to lean forward and put it on the edge of his desk.

Her perfume fit her with its sassy, flirty scent that made his gut clench with heat.

He rose when she moved back to her seat and, taking her hands in his, he brought her to a standing position. Her tongue darted out and dampened her bottom lip, bringing his attention back to her mouth and all the pleasure it could give a man.

Just having her in his sights triggered a hunger in him that ached to be fed.

"I want to work along with you, Christien. I'll go crazy if I have to sit at home and worry."

"Working with you only has one problem. I don't know if I can keep my hands off you," he said.

Tally smiled and Christien's chest tightened at the seduction in those upturned lips eliciting an internal kind of heat. His pulse kicked into high gear and he managed, just barely, to remain outwardly composed.

She arched her lovely brows and said, "Who says I want you to keep your hands off me?"

"I've wanted you ever since I saw you that first

time at Café Eros. I've gotten the impression that you weren't interested."

"It's true. I tried to deny it, but I can't anymore. I'm tired of fighting it, not with everything else going on."

She slipped her arms around him and it was sheer heaven to finally have her willing.

"About your brother, do you know where he lives?"

"I can do better than that," Tally said. "I have his key."

"WHAT A MESS," Tally said when she opened the door and saw the state of her brother's apartment. "It smells like dirty socks in here."

"Bachelor living," Christien said, but she could see a change in him, subtle but noticeable. She'd never seen Christien as anything but charming, though this new facet of his personality caused her to rethink. Obviously, he couldn't be as one-dimensional as she'd thought him to be.

This was strangely disappointing to her. A roll in the sheets with a shallow charmer was one thing, but a man with layers would involve Tally's emotions. Could very well derail her plans for pursuit of what she considered the most important thing in her life: finding Dampier's treasure.

"I hope your place doesn't look like this," Tally said.

"Nope. I'm a neatnik."

Christien went over to the hall table where Mark had dumped his mail. He picked up an envelope. "This is dated five days ago."

"So he hasn't been back here, you think?" Tally said as she surreptitiously looked for any sign of the treasure map. She felt extremely guilty, but it would at least give them a clue as to whether or not her brother had been back to his apartment.

"Not necessarily. He could have come back. A lot of people don't pick up their mail daily."

Christien moved out of the living room and into the bedroom. "Can you tell if any of his clothes are gone? Suitcases?"

"No. I'm not sure. I don't know what he uses to travel."

"Okay. Let's go talk to his neighbors."

Unfortunately, when they knocked on the doors on either side of Mark's apartment, no one answered.

"That's okay. We'll come back later," Christien stated.

"I have to get home and get ready for my shift at Café Eros."

"When do you get off?"

"Six, but I sing at The Blue Note tonight."

"I can—"

"No, I want to be with you on every step of the investigation." Tally needed to be there when he found her brother.

"Okay. When are you finished singing?"

"At ten."

"We can start making the rounds to some of the band hangouts and see what we come up with," Christien suggested. "Did you drive your car over to my office?"

"No, I walked."

"I'll drop you back to Court du Chaud."

Back at the court, Tally leaned over and kissed Christien on the cheek. "Thanks so much for helping me."

When he colored, Tally couldn't help but laugh. The devilish man did have some endearing qualities.

CHRISTIEN WATCHED TALLY from the center table in a packed room. All conversation died as she walked out to the microphone and prepared to sing. It brought his attention to her graceful hands with the red-tipped fingernails, a spotlight refracting the various shades of warm coffee and chocolate richness in her upswept hair that left the long column of her elegant neck bare except for a ruby teardrop that nestled in her cleavage.

She opened her mouth and it seemed as if she sang about the very fever that had consumed him before he'd made his way over here. It was as if time hadn't just stood still, it had slipped deliciously backward.

Her rendition transported him to an era long before anyone had ever thought of SUVs or smart bombs, when people slow-danced and said ma'am, and electricity was something that sparkled between lovers. With a stand-up bass, light brushes on a snare drum and lilting acoustic guitar framing Tally's candlelit jazzy vocals, she breathed new life into the ghosts of torch singers long since past.

The red dress she wore glittered under the bright lights, hugging dangerous curves. From the deep V-halter neckline that shaped her breasts and left her entire back bare to the flattering sheath that cupped her hips. A long sexy slit played peekaboo with her creamy thigh each time she moved.

Christien was charmed and smitten, tension and need coiling tight within him.

He wanted this woman who could transform herself from a hardworking waitress to this…siren.

She finished her set, speaking softly into the microphone in response to the vigorous clapping, "Thank you very much."

She set the microphone on the stand and left the stage, making a direct beeline to his table.

"Just let me change and we can get going."

She disappeared into the back of the restaurant and reemerged twenty minutes later dressed in jeans, a red T-shirt and a denim jacket.

They spent the rest of the evening moving from club to club and talking to anybody who might know where her brother was. A couple of people had seen him, but they couldn't remember if it had been four days ago or when. Discouraged, Tally allowed Christien to take her home.

He insisted on walking her all the way across the court. As they passed the piazza, she noticed the Christmas tree had been taken down. She missed its glittering lights and beauty. At that moment, Christien settled his hand against her lower back. She wasn't keen on men guiding her or hanging on to her, but when Christien touched her it was like those same multicolored fireworks went off underneath her skin.

At her door, she felt his presence with a keenness, the need for comfort strong. She was heartily disappointed that they couldn't find Mark tonight. Time was ticking away and she was beginning to despair. The thought of spending time with a warm body to distract her from her anxieties seemed like shelter from the storm.

"Would you like to come in for a drink?"

"Yes, I would."

Once they were in the town house, Tally chose a bottle of pinot noir. She uncorked it and poured the liquid into glasses.

"Cheers," she said as she toasted with him and drank the dark wine.

Christien didn't drink. He stepped closer to her, the heat from his body mingling with hers.

"Don't be discouraged, Tally. We'll find him. I'm very good at my job."

"I believe you. But I'll feel better when I know he's okay."

"Chances are he's just fine."

"Can you stay a little while?"

"All night long."

His dark eyes sparked with mischief as he stepped closer to her. Fingers fanned wide, he skimmed her jaw, her throat, the slope of her shoulders. Placing small kisses across her eyelids, along her jawline, his mouth explored her slowly.

Every sense was heightened. Every sense was filled. The hardness of his muscles. The sound of breath catching. His dark, thick lashes as they swept against his cheeks. The planes and angles of his beard-shadowed jaw. Tally soaked it up greedily, unaware that a man could make her feel so delicate, so beautiful with just his clever mouth.

Tally savored the strong feel of his arms around her, the sweetness of his kiss. Her skin alive with awareness, she tingled at the slightest brush of his fingertips, the sensations swirling through her like a trail of stardust.

He cradled her breast, his fingers hot and rough through the thin fabric as he pinched her nipple, causing her to gasp out loud. He caught the sound against his mouth. Their lips melded, moved with a pressure that could only be quenched by the taste of the other. His touch flowed downward, over her ribs to her waist, along the flare of her hips.

"Let's go upstairs," Tally said softly against his mouth.

The knock on the door was like cold water against hot skin. Christien sighed and settled his forehead against hers. His dark, slumberous eyes opened. "I'm beginning to believe in voodoo."

"I think you're right."

Tally disengaged herself, already feeling the deprivation of his arms, his touch, his mouth. Yet, when she opened the door and saw her sister's face, it all faded.

"What's wrong, Bree?"

"I woke up from a terrible nightmare where Mark was in trouble."

As soon as Bree saw Christien standing in Tally's

kitchen, his hair mussed, his eyes somnolent and filled with every wicked thing they'd just done, she covered her mouth and said, "Oh, my gosh, I've done it again." She turned to Tally. "I'm so sorry. I came over to ask you if you've seen him lately."

"No. As a matter of fact, I haven't heard from him for five days."

"Why didn't you tell me?"

"I didn't want to worry you, too. I guess I thought he'd show up."

"Don't worry, Bree," Christien said, tucking in his shirt and shrugging back into his jacket. "I'm helping Tally find him." He walked into the foyer and put a hand on Tally's shoulder. Looking at her, he grinned and she felt the warmth shoot right through her.

"I'll see you tomorrow."

"Okay."

When the door closed, Bree turned apologetic and worried eyes to her sister. "I swear, Tally. I don't know why I came over here and didn't wait until tomorrow. I just felt compelled."

Tally looked around her town house and shivered. Was there some malevolent force at work here?

4

GABRIEL WATCHED TALLY with her sister. Dealing with one twin at a time would be enough for him. For now. He would deal with Bree later. Although, he couldn't appear to Tally since he was having the devil's own time becoming visible and remaining that way.

Bree kissed her sister's cheek and said, "Good night, Tally. Sweet dreams. Let's hope we hear from Mark soon."

At the last minute, Tally called out, "Don't forget about the krewe meeting tomorrow night."

"We just had a krewe meeting," Bree's grumbled.

"That was last week," Tally said, rolling her eyes. "We have them every week." As soon as Bree left, Gabriel willed himself to move from the incorporeal to the corporeal world. But it was to no avail as Tally passed right through him.

"Tally," he said, but she didn't pause. This idea of materializing was probably one of the old crone's many ways to trick him and watch him suffer.

"What is it you're trying to do, Gabriel?" Her voice dripped with smug contempt.

"Go away, old woman, and leave me to my own misery."

Tally dumped the wine out of the glasses and rinsed them under the faucet, oblivious to their conversation.

"You are trying to appear to her, are you not?"

"Aye, but I am finding it very difficult. Go ahead and gloat."

"Whether you appear to her or not will not do you any good, but I guess I could give you a hint."

"Why would you do that?"

"There is no sport in this paltry attempt of yours to win your redemption. If you neglect to even talk to the girl, how can you participate? Your misery will be even more delicious once you fail."

"Give me the hint, old woman, and then begone. I have no patience for you this night."

"Taking what you lack is the key."

He stood there for a moment.

"Think about it, thick skull. It's a wonder you ever found your way out of your house let alone plan the liberation of New Orleans."

"Saving a city was child's play compared to this...this manipulation of emotions."

"There is no manipulation, Gabriel. When a woman's heart is open, she will fall for the man who is destined for her." She bit her lip.

Gabriel realized that she'd said more than she'd meant to. He had to take his triumphs where he found them. "Aha! Christien is her destined match?"

Pinching her face into a tight frown, she threw her shawl around her throat with a flourish. "I have given you enough ammunition, pirate. Work with that, if you can."

Gabriel gave the crone a dismissive look and turned away, no longer able to tolerate her smug piercing eyes. Take what you lack? She would be a hag and make him muddle through riddles. If he could get a headache, one would be blooming behind his eyes right now.

So, take what he lacked. Well, that was easy. He lacked substance. Materialize meant substance. To become solid. But how?

He wanted to move on. He was sick of this purgatory, of seeing and hearing people and not being a part of life, reminding him constantly of the life he'd squandered and the cruel death that had taken away any chance he'd had of making amends. What he could not attain in life, he was determined to accomplish in death. Closure.

Tally was only half of his ticket. If he couldn't figure out a way to materialize to Tally, he couldn't hope to affect her life, make her see that her ambition was nothing but cold ash compared to the hot embers of love. Without Tally, he would forever be trapped in hell with that thrice-cursed old crone!

He scrutinized every inch of what stood before him. For over two hundred years since he'd been trapped in this limbo, caught between life and death, he'd seen this old house go from candlelight to electricity.

He looked at the lightbulb that was burning in the living room. With slow footsteps, he walked toward it. It had an aura as all things with power had—hair driers, electric shavers, television sets and microwave ovens. Could he tap into these sources? After all, the human body's aura was made up of electromagnetic power.

Is that what the crone was talking about?

He reached out and just tried to absorb the energy pulsing from the bulb. He felt a strange sensation, like the tingles one got when leaning on a limb too long. He turned toward the stairs and said, "Tally!"

This time, she stopped and turned around, but, although his voice carried, she still could not see him. "Double blasted damn," he swore as Tally stared into the gloom at the bottom of the stairs. He would have to work harder.

OKAY, TALLY THOUGHT. Was her imagination playing tricks on her or did she just hear someone call her name? It was a man's voice, a voice she didn't recognize.

Tally had only lived in Court du Chaud for a year, but in all that time, she'd neither seen nor heard Captain Dampier's ghost. Now, in the span of a week, she'd seen him twice and, right now, she was relatively certain that he had been calling her name.

What could have changed the status quo to make him try to contact her? She searched around in gloom for a few minutes. When nothing happene she started to feel stupid. She turned and continued up the stairs. Pretty soon people were going to call her *eccentric* if she were to breathe a word about the ghost or the treasure.

Was she destined to be the court's crackpot?

Chloe had all but said everyone thought her uncle was crazy, but she knew that Chloe believed in the ghost. It was the treasure everyone thought was a bunch of bunk.

Was she playing into the lure of the treasure to obtain what she'd always wanted? Something to call her own, stability she'd lacked in her childhood? She could easily blame her mother for these feelings.

Poor Linda had always been searching for an easy

out and along the way had left a trail of men and tears. Her mother had thrown obstacles in the way of her own happiness and robbed her daughters of the same in her vain search for a quick and easy payoff for some get-rich-quick scheme.

Tally wasn't much interested in following in her mother's footsteps when it came to love or money. Surely, she was different. She intended to bring her plans to fruition and she was certain that she was on the right track. She still had a week to find Mark and the treasure map.

Thinking about finding Mark brought her inevitably back to Christien. Fully male, full of himself and so irresistible. She promised herself she would not get caught up in emotions and certainly not fall in love with the sexy rogue, but enjoying his body and his outrageous behavior was something she could quite happily do. Although, she did have to admit he'd been so sweet to her this afternoon. She couldn't help a small bit of guilt as it slipped in like an unwanted guest.

She hoped Mark wasn't in any danger. She did care about him.

But she had to find that map.

She had every right.

After all, a ghost wanted her to have it.

And have it she would.

She looked back to the area where she'd seen the captain. "I will succeed," she said softly, rubbing at the goose bumps that rose along her arms.

She dressed for bed, feeling as if unseen eyes were watching her. She knew she was being silly, but the deep, dark night seemed to press in on her.

She longed suddenly for strong arms around her and a warm, living man telling her in a beautifully accented voice there were no such things as ghosts. Her body ached for touch and closeness, for the simple sound of a man's easy breathing.

She got into bed and after a few minutes of lying in the inky darkness, she got up and turned on the bathroom light, pulling the door closed until it was a bright sliver in the darkness. Getting back into bed, she closed her eyes, the warm glow of the light comforting.

"THROW ME THE BEADS. Me! Here I am! Throw them to me!" Tally said as she reached out with her hands, but the gaily painted beads slipped through her fingers like brightly colored lights.

She tried to bend down to scoop them from the pavement, but something held on to her, pulling her back, stifling her hope, bringing with it a despair that only made her tug harder. And Captain Dampier's float moved by, his handsome face slowly replaced by that of a malevolent clown, his cruel expression telling her that, like him, she'd never get what she so richly deserved.

Her alarm clock went off, the lively strains of Mary Chapin Carpenter singing about going to the Twist and Shout for a hurricane party and dancing to a Cajun beat.

Tally sang the refrain, letting the ugly images of her dream fade.

In the bathroom, she took care of her morning ablutions. Back in the bedroom, she pulled open a drawer to get dressed for the day. Heavy knocking at her front door made her wonder who could be here first thing in the morning. She grabbed her robe and went downstairs.

Christien Castille and his brother Jack stood there looking as much alike as she and Bree. Both men were wonderful to see. But more than their physical attributes captured her attention. There were edges to Christien that he made no effort to hide, and there were auras of strength and power surrounding them, as if in any crisis these men could be counted on to take control.

They hadn't gained that presence by years in law enforcement, Tally knew that instinctively. Something terrible had shaped these men, had left indelible marks on their psyches.

"Hello Christien, Jack. You two are easy to look

at first thing in the morning, but why am I looking at you?"

"We've come to help you take care of your damaged cypress floor."

"In through here?" Jack asked, grasping two pieces of cypress wood in his hand. Christien nodded and Christien's brother—Chloe's boyfriend—walked into her house.

She grabbed Christien by his shirt front, drawing him down close to her face. "How long did it take you to find those pieces? I've been looking since the floor got damaged."

He grinned and Tally felt as if her insides turned to pure liquid.

"Not long. I have a friend who was renovating. I asked and he said yes."

"I didn't expect this kind of help."

"Help is something you give, not something you ask for." He looked at her face like a man who was very hungry, his dark eyes warm and filled with the devil's own mischief. "Besides, I suspect the shock waves from that kiss we shared caused it to fall. Makes me liable for some of the damages."

"Christien, that's absurd—"

He put his fingers over her mouth, the heat effectively scorching her body and silencing her.

"Sounded so good to me when I thought it up this

morning, I roused my grumpy brother out of bed. Got him away from his sexy girlfriend."

"All to help me, sugar? How come I'm suspicious?"

"Of me?" he said, his eyes gleaming with amusement.

"Fess up why you're really here."

"Ah, Tally, you still don't know." He leaned forward and whispered in her ear. "I'm hot for you."

"I'm hot for you, too."

He laughed and grabbed her around the waist and brought her hard against him.

This time it was her turn to lean forward. She captured his earlobe and bit down gently, smiling when he gasped. "Sugar, I'm a sure thing."

"You do feel pretty solid to me."

At the sound of Jack's raised voice and a stream of Cajun, Christien grimaced.

"He said something bad?" Tally said.

"*Mais* yeah."

Jack appeared at the entrance to the foyer. "Christien, get over here and give me a hand. You're the one who got me out of bed."

"See, told you. Grumpy."

Jack looked at Tally. "He promised me breakfast, too."

Christien slipped past her, but not before she slapped him on his gorgeous butt. "Then you'll get it."

Jack nodded and turned to go. Tally said, "Jack." He faced her. "Thanks."

They spent a couple of hours pulling up the damaged board and replacing it. Tally watched them work companionably smiling at how close they were, how well they worked together.

When Christien caught her watching him, he flashed her a grin. Overwhelmed by his generosity her heart turned over in her chest. Who was this man? Surely not the guy she'd thought him to be. So far she had been way off base.

Tally was speechless. "You didn't have to do this," she said after she'd fed them both and Jack had left.

"It would have cost you a bundle to get a guy in here to do it. Are you afraid the present comes with strings attached?"

"No. I thought we'd come to an agreement on that. I don't like to owe anyone."

"When it's a present, owing doesn't fit into the equation."

This man was irresistible when it came to just about everything. What could it hurt if she accepted a small gift from him? "Okay. Thanks."

He nodded. "See. Was that so hard?"

"No," she laughed in spite of herself. "It wasn't." After a moment, she said, "I called Chloe and told her I'd be late. I should get going."

He nodded again. The gleam in his dark eyes enticed her. He moved closer. "Christien, I have to get to work."

"I know. Just one little kiss?" That clever, sexy mouth curled up at the corners.

"With you nothing is little."

The smile deepening, the magnetism pulling harder, he leaned a little closer. "Ain't that the truth," he murmured. "Absolutely. Guar-un-teed."

Tally gave up her hold on her sense of humor and chuckled, shaking her head. "You're impossible."

"Oh, no," he teased, slipping his arms around her once again. "I'm the easy in The Big Easy."

The innuendo was unmistakable and outrageous. It hit Tally on two levels—one that turned her internal temperature up a notch and one that made her laugh out loud. Christien laughed with her, then their gazes caught, and the two levels of invisible contact met, meshed, pushed together, rising into another plane entirely.

Their laughter drifted away on the sultry air and awareness thickened around them. Tally felt her heart thump a little harder as she watched the rogue's mask fall away from Christien's face. He looked intense, but it was a softer look than she had seen there before, and when he smiled, it was a softer smile, a smile that made her breath catch in her throat.

"I like your laugh, *chère*," he said, lifting a hand to touch her hair. His fingers slid down her cheek, grazed the corner of her mouth and cupped her chin. Slowly, he tilted her face up as he lowered his mouth to hers.

Excitement burst through Tally—those fireworks again. Her lips softened beneath his and his arms felt so good when they slipped around her. It was true. She wasn't looking for a relationship. Yet, she couldn't have found a better candidate for some fun between the sheets. Christien Castille was wild and irreverent and unpredictable. The fire that sparked to life as he tightened his hold on her and eased his tongue into her mouth defied all her arguments.

He broke the kiss to stare into her face. "Think Chloe would miss you for another half hour?"

"I think she's pretty smart, Christien. She'll notice."

"But the question that begs to be asked is will you care?"

"Are you saying I'll be so besotted with you that I'm willing to lose more money? I'm not so sure you're worth it."

With one-hundred-percent-male cockiness, Christien picked up the silky belt to her robe and let it run through his fingers. "Tally, I'm more than worth it. Let me prove it to you."

He deftly untied her robe before she could utter another word.

"I, uh—" The look in his eye and the way the silk slid through his fingers stripped her of every witty comeback she could think of. The very idea of both silk and those rough and rugged hands of his caressing her skin at the same time left her speechless. Not to mention a bit breathless.

He pushed the robe off her shoulders and it floated down to pool like liquid passion. "You look real good in red, Tally, but I'd bet you'd look even better in nothing, *chère,*" he breathed, eyes full of mischief…and a few other things.

Things that had her clearing her throat, suddenly desperate for a sip of water. Or him. "I, uh—"

"You know, you'll need to work on that speech problem you seem to be having." He stroked her hair, her face. "It won't be as much fun taking advantage of you if you don't fight back."

"You don't play fair, Christien," she said, regaining her footing. Something about his gleaming eyes stirred her tongue…and other body parts.

"Can't afford to. I need the upper hand with you," he said, quite seriously.

"Oh, Christien, you'll need to use both hands with me."

His grin went blistering hot. "Ah, there's that sharp tongue of yours. I want it now."

Her pulse spiked. "Really?"

He pressed closer. "Absolutely."

"Too impatient to wait for a formal invitation?"

"I don't believe in proper etiquette."

"Well, isn't that a nice little coincidence?" she said, "Neither do I."

He smoothed his hands up her torso, shifting the silk of her nightgown along her ribs, sliding the fabric over her tingling nipples.

He bent over and took one into his mouth.

She jerked at the feel of him, at the wet heat next to her skin. "Christien," she whispered and then moaned as he slowly moved to her other nipple.

"I think I'm going to get hard every time I look at red silk."

She stared down at him, then let her eyes drift shut and her head tip back as he went back to tasting raw silk...and naked Tally.

Christien moaned when the phone rang. "I bet that's Chloe," Tally murmured.

"Or Mark?"

She quickly sobered at the thought of her brother still missing and The Blue Note going on the block very soon.

She extricated herself from Christien's embrace and reached for the phone.

Feeling a boatload of regret at the timing of the call, she said, "Hello."

Static crackled in her ear.

5

IT WASN'T MARK.

Later Christien wondered, as he approached his apartment, whether it was possible to die from boredom. Mostly he'd been doing a number of background checks for a business client. Talking to his former colleague Jim Carter and getting information on Sarah Richardson's mother's killer was the only interesting part of his day.

He couldn't seem to make a difference when he'd been a cop and it still irked him that he'd left the department the way he had, but he wasn't sorry for decking the guy in the courtroom.

He did regret quitting, but it had been his decision not to return to the force. Jack had said he was cutting off his nose to spite his face, but Christien had felt he could do more good if he became a P.I.

Unfortunately, that hadn't happened. He spent most of his time doing research and taking on divorce cases. Finding Mark was as close to police work as he could get.

Now, all Christien wanted was to strip off his clothes, take a shower and then find Tally. He'd rather spend a whole lot of hours trying to get Tally Addison out of her clothes and into his bed, but her brother was missing and that had to take precedence.

Christien had used some of his day to return to Mark's apartment to see if he could get any kind of clue about where the man might be. He'd discovered a flyer for a band called the Emoticons who were scheduled to play at a club called the Spirit of Fluxus. The club was named after a style of music called Fluxus. The Fluxus movement advocated a shift from aesthetics to ethics in artistic values. It'd be as good as anyplace to start their search for Mark's whereabouts.

Glancing at his watch, he realized that Tally was going to be at his apartment in half an hour.

As he finished his short, hot shower, a knock sounded at the door and he hastily wrapped a towel around his waist.

He sucked in a breath at the sight of Tally dressed in a stretchy lace skirt, lined in red Lycra that hugged her curves, a black halter and a short red leather jacket.

"You'll cause quite a stir in that outfit," she said

as she strolled into the apartment with a sexy roll of her hips, her short black boot heels clicking against his old wood floor.

"Nah, I'm not wearing this, too drafty."

She smiled, her delectable red-painted mouth looking very kissable.

She put her hand up. "Oh, no. Get that look off your face. We have to stay focused on finding my brother."

He released a harsh exhale. "Am I that transparent?"

"You get this I'm-going-to-ravish-you look in your eye. I have to tell you, it's very effective."

It was his turn to smile as he went into his bedroom, leaving the door ajar.

Dropping the towel and grabbing white briefs and a pair of black jeans out of the chest of drawers, he dressed his lower half.

Threading a black belt through the loops of his jeans, he left the bedroom and headed to the adjacent bathroom to dry his hair. Tally had been looking at his wall of family pictures. She moved across the room and sat on his couch.

Her eyes tracked his progress. They caressed his chest, flowing down his body to his groin. Taking in her hungry gaze, he vowed that he would have her beneath him before this night was through, but searching for her brother came first.

He shot her a wicked grin, one she responded to by rolling her eyes and releasing a quick breath.

"You're put together very nicely, Mr. Castille, but you're not the sum of your gorgeous parts." Her gaze deepened, meeting his in a head-on collision. "No matter how much you might want me to think so."

A little frisson of surprise sizzled up his spine. Did he want this woman to see what was beneath the cocky grin and the devil-may-care attitude he carried around like a cloak to mask the dedicated core inside himself? Only his family really knew who he was. Had he exposed himself to her so she saw something more? She was a complicated woman; a woman who needed her independence, yet at times seemed so vulnerable it hurt his heart. He found that so much more of a turn-on than her physical features. He had no snappy comeback, so he took the coward's way out and ducked into the bathroom.

Hair dried and pulled back, Christien went into the bedroom to slip a green long-sleeved henley over his head. He then donned socks and a pair of boots.

"Before we go, let me give you an update." He picked up and opened a notebook, revealing his attempt to keep all his cases organized. He flipped to a tabbed section marked Tally, which contained pages of notes. "I checked to see if your brother booked any international or domestic flights."

Tally sat forward, uncrossing her long bare legs. "What did you find out?"

"Nothing on that, unfortunately." He thumbed through a few pages and skimmed over more written information. "I also managed to check the charges on his credit cards to see if he'd purchased a ticket from some other source, and again no luck."

"So you think he's still in New Orleans?"

"Not necessarily, Tally. He could have gone on someone else's tab or driven out of the city."

The distress was evident on her face and Christien switched places and sat down next to her on the couch to give her the rest of what he'd found out. He slipped his arm around her shoulders. "Tally, he hasn't accessed any money, which is very odd. When someone goes away, he takes money with him."

"Do you think something has happened to him?"

He squeezed her shoulders. The unexpected sense of loss struck him. He knew what it was like to lose someone you loved. "No, Tally. Don't do that to yourself. I'm reporting everything I found to you."

"I appreciate that, Christien," she said, laying her head on his shoulder and burrowing her face into his neck.

And his heart turned over, that small gesture latching on to his heart and squeezing tight.

As if she realized suddenly what she was doing,

she stiffened and pulled away. "We should get going."

Unsettled by his own reaction to Tally, he nodded and rose from the couch.

Once in his Jeep, Tally asked, "So where are we going tonight?"

"To the Spirit of Fluxus," he said. The targeted club, only a year old, was located not far from Tou-jacques Casino. A very convenient establishment for bored party animals attracted to the jazz, food and frivolity of clubbing in the Vieux Carré. A few blocks away they could immerse themselves in the equally dazzling pull of slot machines and blackjack.

"Where?"

Christien's eyes shifted from the road. "Do you and your brother have a rocky relationship?"

"Not rocky, no. It's just like any other sibling relationship."

"I went back to his apartment to search again and he had a flyer tacked up on his fridge for a band that's playing at that club," Christien said.

Tally's gaze swung away from his. "I have no idea what my brother's tastes in music are. Right now that seems wrong. I realize that I'm negative most of the time."

"What's the beef you're having with your brother?"

"Bree and I want him to go to college. Instead he runs around and sets up for bands. At least I think that's what he does."

He lifted his brows and she frowned.

"I didn't like what he did, so I didn't pay attention," she said, a defensive note creeping into her voice.

"Maybe that's why he's shutting you out of his life."

"Look, when you raise a sibling, you can chastise me."

"You raised your brother?"

"Bree and I did. He was fourteen when my mother up and left and never came back. Mark had to fend for himself for four days before he got nervous and called us."

"And you were all of…eighteen?"

"Nineteen. I was in my first semester at Stanford and Bree was at Duke. I quit school at the time to care for Mark."

"Quit? Why didn't you bring Mark to Stanford with you and live off-campus?"

"It was complicated. Mom just left and, unfortunately, she left us with her debt. I couldn't pay for school and pay off the money she owed. I always planned to go back. Bree quit Duke a semester later when I could barely make ends meet. We needed the double income to support our brother."

"So Stanford, huh?"

"Yeah. Why? Does it surprise you?"

"Just another intriguing layer that makes up Tally. What did you major in?"

"Business."

"Really?"

"That also surprises you?"

"You don't look like the business type."

"What type do I look like?"

"Artsy."

"Art's an iffy profession. It takes a lot of talent and a lot of work to make it. There's no guarantee of security."

"Doing what you love isn't always about security."

"I don't have the luxury of doing what I love, Christien."

"How did you end up in Court du Chaud?"

"About a year ago, my uncle Guidry died and left the town house to us. Bree and I renovated it."

"Your uncle? Crazy old man Guidry? Jack told me about him."

"Yes, and he wasn't crazy."

"Sorry. That was out of line."

"He was convinced that the ghost of Dampier haunted the court and wasn't afraid to tell anyone about it. He also believed there's a large cache of treasure he insists the captain hid."

"If you're Guidry's niece that makes you a descendent of Dampier."

"Yes and I'm proud to be. I've…ah, done some research on him and started to collect anything I could find about him. I intend to make sure he takes his place in history. He assisted Lafitte, and saved New Orleans from the British. If the British troops had reached the city proper, they would have burned it to the ground."

"I have nothing against rogues as long as they don't break the law in my city."

"He bent the rules, but the fact remains that if it wasn't for him, the city would have been lost."

"Sounds like you really admire this guy?"

"I think he deserves a place in history, yes. I intend to see that he gets it."

"I like that you're on a crusade for a pirate."

Tally gave him a narrow look. "Yeah, I seem to have a soft spot for scalawags."

Christien chuckled. "I've never been a scalawag in my life, but I did get into my share of mischief. I got a kick out of shocking and pissing people off. Most of the time, Jack bailed me out."

"I got the feeling you were a troublemaker from day one. Your mother must have had her hands full."

"My mother died twenty years ago yesterday."

Christien turned into a parking space next to a

small brick building with a neon sign proclaiming Spirit of Fluxus. The lot looked nearly full, but he eventually found a parking spot at the farthest end. He turned off the ignition. Silence filled the car. Finally, he turned to her.

"Yesterday. Is that why you weren't in your office?" Tally asked.

"I was putting flowers on my mother's grave."

"Oh." Tally shifted in her seat and didn't look at him. "I guess we should go in."

Talking about his mother's death wasn't as hard as it used to be, but he was still surprised that Tally didn't mouth the usual platitudes. In fact, she seemed in a hurry to drop the subject.

For a moment, it looked like she was going to say something else, but then she opened her door and stepped out of his Jeep. Heading toward the main entrance, he jogged to catch up with her. She slung her purse over her shoulder as she made her way briskly across the blacktop.

Christien hung back, aware of how beautifully she moved. After a short wait, they walked through the doors and into a dark, smoky interior shot through with colored lights that streaked and arced erratically from one end to the other.

At the moment, no live band was playing on the small stage, only a DJ playing music. The DJ was lost in his work, jamming to the tunes and oblivious to the frenzied light show. Synthesized, percussion-heavy music assaulted Christien's ears, so loud the pounding beat vibrated through his body.

The current choice was a husky-voiced female growling something about lust. It fit with his mood.

Feeling ten times more protective and a hundred times more possessive, Christien took Tally's arm when he saw all the guys at the bar ogling her.

He sat down and Tally followed suit. When the bartender came over, Christien ordered two beers and pulled Mark's photo from his wallet. "Have you seen this guy around here lately?"

"I don't know. Why? You a cop?"

"No. I'm not a cop and he isn't in any trouble. He's this woman's brother and we're tying to find him. He had a flyer for a band who's supposed to be playing later on."

"Right. The Emoticons. They won't be here until eleven."

"This guy work for them?"

The guy rubbed the back of his neck and shook his head. "Naw, sorry. I can't place him." He set the beers on the bar. "That'll be nine bucks."

Christien paid and turned toward Tally's disappointed expression. "Looks like we wait for the band."

"Looks like it."

It wasn't much more than an open room with a bar and a scattering of tall tables to one side and a stage on the other, a sizable dance floor sandwiched between the two. The ceiling was bare with exposed pipes, ducts and metal beams hung with lights and speakers. A metal, retro-modern balcony circled the main room, with platforms that held tables and chairs.

The funky balcony would be a great lookout place for checking out the action below. "Let's get up there. We'll have a better view," Christien shouted over the music.

Tally nodded.

Once on the main balcony, he searched out a spot that provided the best view of the club, as well as the rest of the balcony. He would have preferred an area less crowded, but didn't have a lot of options. Below, he scanned the room for any sign of Tally's brother on the off chance he would appear.

There was an eclectic mishmash of clothing. While some wore casual clothes, others wore more punk studs, buckles, black fingernail polish and piercings. The flashing laser lights, in multiple colors, lanced through a thin haze of smoke, and the music was so loud the metal railing and balcony throbbed beneath his hands and feet.

Yet he saw no one who met her brother's description.

Tally vibrated with frustration as she searched the crowd as avidly as Christien, hoping for her brother to make an appearance. Her time was running out and soon the Blue Note would be sold.

The restaurant/lounge was the ultimate culmination of her plan and now it was in total jeopardy. She felt sick with the fear that she would end up just like her mother. Empty promises, empty life.

That some day she would bail on the people she loved because of all her ugly failures and broken promises.

The treasure was everything. Everything! It would give her what she'd always wanted and the only thing she really needed.

Security.

Christien moved and his distracting scent had her turning her head to get more of a whiff of him. The sight of him dressed only in his towel had stirred her blood. All that muscle in stark relief built a sweet ache inside her. She remembered she had told Chloe how she'd wanted to run her hands all over him.

A nearby couple was making out; the man had his mouth and hands all over the woman and she unabashedly participated. Tally tried not to watch them, but she couldn't help it. They were right in her line of vision. The man and woman were completely lost in each other, kissing and rubbing and touching... and it reminded her, with a pang of envy, how much she missed kissing and making love. It had been a while since her ex-boyfriend had walked out on her, unable to deal with her workaholic ways.

What was she waiting for? Christien stood next to her making her totally aware of him just by breathing. He was big and warm and looked delicious, the red of his shirt accentuating the darkness of his hair.

"Don't that boy need to breathe?" Christien's amused rough-and-tumble drawl was so close against her ear, a shiver coursed through her.

Tally turned to him. A wave of desire washed over her. He was watching her intently, with a heat that played havoc with her equilibrium and stirred a blend of chaotic, inconvenient responses.

"How long can you hold your breath, sugar?"

He smiled at her. It was a slow, sensuous, utterly male smile of invitation and longing that clearly came from the depths of him and radiated in his eyes.

Tally was unprepared for the small shock that gripped her when his fingers slipped to the nape of her neck. She was even more unsettled by the gentleness of his touch, his power under exquisite control. A woman would always be aware of the strength in this man, she thought, but she would never fear it.

His fingertips moved once more across the nape of her neck, stirring the fine hair that grew there. Tally shivered.

Stepping closer, he cupped the back of her head and with very little pressure brought his mouth down on hers. She moaned softly, the touch of his mouth wildly disorienting, a riot of color for her senses. When both of his hands closed around her, she caught her breath. His warmth and strength reached out to capture her and pull her into a glittering trap. All the fascination, the physical awareness and the underlying compulsion to know Christien that had been unsettling her for days swamped her now.

She knew he was aware of her reaction. It made her feel vulnerable, and for a moment some of her wariness returned.

"Vous me voulez," he said, his mouth brushing her own.

She knew enough French to translate the words. He'd said, "You want me."

"Je vous veux," she responded and he gave her a surprised but pleased smile. When his thumb touched the corner of her lips and urged a response, she moaned softly. She opened her mouth to him and braced herself for the invasion of his tongue.

It was subtle when it came, not a rush at her defenses, but a careful, enticing dance that left her shivering. It was only as he slowly filled her mouth, tasting her intimately, that she began to realize just how thorough his ultimate possession would be.

He reluctantly broke the kiss as soon as the DJ stopped.

For a moment, she looked into his dark and sensual eyes and was afraid he would see the longing in hers, but all she encountered was a desire that mirrored her own.

From their vantage point, they could see the band roll in, but the person setting up for them wasn't Mark.

"I'm going down to talk to the band. I'll be right back," Christien said.

"I'll go with you."

"I think it's better if you stay here. One person asking questions is enough to spook them. We don't want them to clam up."

"Okay."

Below, Christien crossed the full expanse of the bar. Tally watched as a number of women stopped him, smiling and flirting. Christien nodded to them, but gave them no encouragement. Tally hadn't realized how hard she'd gripped the metal rail beneath her palms or the flash of what she could only call jealousy.

She released the bar, letting that emotion flow out

of her. Christien was a free agent. She had no hold over him and didn't want one. He would be spectacular in bed and that was all that interested Tally.

He stopped in front of the stage. She watched as Christien talked to one of the band members and showed him Mark's picture. Tally's heart soared and started to pound as the guy nodded his head and spoke to Christien.

She waited with bated breath as he made his way back across the floor, the very same women trying to get his attention, but all she felt now was irritation. When he finally got to the balcony, Tally said, "Have they seen him?"

"Yes, a few days ago and…ah…"

"What?"

"He was complaining about you."

"Was he?"

"Tally, have you considered that he could be dodging you?"

Tally blinked, shocked at the sting in her eyes. She looked away. Knowing that Mark resented her so much hurt Tally to the very core of who she was. "I guess that's possible."

She felt the hot slide of Christien's hand around her nape. Her heart slipped a little when she saw the tenderness in his soft brown eyes.

He nodded in understanding, but his gaze held a

gentleness that tugged at her heart. "He's a kid, Tally, and maybe he's acting immature. Doesn't mean he doesn't love you. Maybe you should give him some time to cool down."

Tally began to pace restlessly—anything to burn off the extra energy building within her. "No. I have to talk to him."

"Riding a guy hard isn't going to get the results you want. Give him some room to find out who he is, he'll come around to your way of thinking."

Tally shrugged. "Seems like Bree and I have all the ambition in the family. Mark doesn't seem to have any."

"You don't know that. He's nineteen. He's young and, for the record, so are you."

"Thanks for that information, Grandpa."

"I'm just saying prodding doesn't work."

"Mark said I was a nag."

"The band didn't use that specific word."

"I'll feel much better if I talk to him, Christien. You'll help me find him, won't you?"

Christien sighed. "The band he's currently working for is called Calendar Boys, but the lead singer downstairs told me they're on the road. He said they'll be back in town tomorrow night."

"You'll help me?"

"Yes, *chère,* I'll help you. I can't seem to say no."

6

"TELL ME YOU HAVE NO INTENTION of sleeping alone tonight," Christien said as soon as the door shut behind them.

His tone set off such a reaction in her that she could barely stay erect, and she closed her eyes trying to bring her wayward feelings under control.

"Tell me what I want to hear." Smiling slightly, he stroked her lip with his thumb, his voice softer, huskier, more seductive.

Mesmerized by the look in his eyes, she somehow managed to swallow, her voice so uneven it didn't sound like her own. "I have no intention of sleeping alone tonight." She tried to tell herself it was different. Need and want. Very different.

"That's good. Would you like a drink?"

The fact that he didn't immediately get right down to sex did unbearable things to her heart, and she closed her eyes against the sudden fullness in her chest.

Christien slid his fingers along her neck, his touch making her shiver; then he rubbed his thumb against her frantically beating pulse point.

Her system overloaded, her pulse heavy, her heart laboring against it.

He'd driven back to his apartment as she'd expected and had asked her to come in, also as she'd expected, but the harsh need in his voice easily took her to a plane of desire that she'd never experienced with any man. Truth of the matter was, no man had ever gotten this close to her.

She always thought of her heart as an impenetrable organ with only enough room for her sister and brother. Had no expectations that she would feel anything for a man like Christien.

Whoa, she had to amend that. For the man she thought Christien was. It was now quite obvious that he wasn't the one-dimensional heartbreaker she'd thought him to be. His admission that he needed her made her nervous and turned her on. She didn't want to be needed.

Being needed came with too many expectations and responsibilities. She was on the cusp of getting everything she wanted, a new life that included a fresh start without anything threatening to destroy her chance at happiness, of being independent and self-reliant. Security was within her grasp.

But craving this new, less complicated life didn't stop Tally from wanting more of Christien. She wanted to know what it was like to be needed by such a man. Shocking that she would feel such an emotional connection to him. Beyond their physical attraction, he made her feel, and it had been a long time, if ever, since anyone had touched her heart and emotions so profoundly. She thought about the things she kept from him—the treasure, the ghost—and knew, for her own self-preservation, she would keep them still. Digging herself in deeper wasn't a rational decision yet she couldn't seem to help herself.

She remembered what he'd said about his mother and, with the resentment she harbored for hers, she wondered how he had handled his own.

"How old were you when your mother died?"

His dark brown eyes were unreadable, giving none of his own thoughts away, which only added to her curiosity about him.

"Six."

Tally had never had a problem keeping eye contact with anyone, yet his straightforward expression got to her and she had to look away. "I'm sorry I didn't ask you about it before, but I have issues with my own mother."

"Why are you asking me about it now?"

"I want to know." She licked her lips. "I want to know about you."

Regretfully, he stepped away and went over to a wet bar in the corner and picked up a bottle of Grand Marnier. He poured the dark amber liquid into two glasses.

"Before you sleep with me? A baring of the souls, Tally?" he uttered in a low, gruff timbre, and his words thrilled and terrified her.

"Yes. How did she die?"

He tipped the glass up and took a sip, his eyes closing as he savored the taste of the potent libation. He walked back to her, settled on the sofa and handed her the other glass. "Robbery. She got in the way."

Tally brought the glass to her lips, the amber liquid on the rim smelling and tasting of sweet oranges. When the liquid hit her tongue, the orange flavor burst against her taste buds, a smooth, sweet and spicy combination. As she savored the aftertaste, she said, "That's terrible."

"I couldn't identify the killer in a lineup."

She fumbled for words, the alcohol souring on her tongue. "You mean you saw it?"

He nodded.

"Oh, Christien, how awful."

He braced his arms on his thighs and clasped his hands together. "The only regret I have is the killer is running around free."

She sat down on the sofa, setting the glass on his coffee table. Slipping her hands over his, an overwhelming urge to hold and soothe him warred with her need to remain detached. "Is that why you became a cop?"

"Yes. Jack and I became cops and Jolie a prosecutor."

She moved closer to him, her hand stealing to the back of his neck, rubbing at his hot skin. "Why aren't you on the force anymore?"

She waited for him to answer as he suddenly leaned into her, rubbing his jaw along her cheekbone. She waited patiently for him to continue, knowing she'd sit there for hours, days, weeks, to learn more about him. It was a dangerous decision, but at the moment, she only cared about him—uncertainties, painful secrets and all.

He closed his eyes for a brief moment, as if remembering; then his lashes lifted. His gaze was distant, as though he were caught somewhere in the past. "I punched out a suspect in court."

Anger? Frustration? His recklessness was an innate part of him, something that simmered just below the surface. She wanted to ask so many questions. "Did you? Wow. What happened to make you lose it so badly?"

He glanced back at her and managed a shaky half

smile, but the gesture was forced over the emotional torment flickering in his eyes. "He smirked at me."

"Smirked?"

"After he was collared for murder, I was sent to his house. His wife let us into his workshop and I found evidence not only from the victim's home, but from three other women who were murdered the same way."

"Don't tell me."

"The evidence got suppressed and we lost the case."

"That's when he smirked at you?"

"And that's when I hit him."

"Did he press charges?"

"He did, but my representative said that I was under stress and he dropped the charges. The perp realized that he wasn't going to get a sympathetic judge. They suspended me, but after my suspension was over, I quit."

"What? Christien, you left a job you love over this incident?"

"I wanted justice."

He seemed so incredibly selfless, at the very heart and soul of who he was. A man who wanted nothing more than for everything around him to be good and right. "So is this guy running around free?"

"Not for long," Christien said roughly.

"What does that mean?"

"My former colleague Jim Carter and I keep tabs on him. Eventually he'll slip up and we'll have him."

"Oh, Christien."

"I want to make a difference."

Feeling like she was drowning in his beautiful brown eyes, she cupped his cheeks. "I don't doubt it for a moment."

He stared at her, his expression strained. Then he tipped her face up and slowly lowered his head, and Tally made a helpless sound and let her eyes drift shut. Exerting pressure on her jaw, he covered her mouth in a wet, deep searching kiss that drove every ounce of strength out of her body.

Leaning back, he pulled her into a hard, enveloping embrace, drawing her between his thighs, working his mouth hungrily against hers, pulling her hips even closer. Tally couldn't breathe, she couldn't think. All she could do was hang on and ride out the thousand sensations exploding in her.

Christien caught her by the hips and molded her flush against him, his mouth wide and hot as he ran his hand under her halter top and up her back. He made a low sound of approval when he discovered nothing but bare skin. Gliding his hand up her bare torso, cupping her breast, he stroked her with his thumb.

His touch made her gasp, and she made another helpless sound against his mouth. Christien tightened his arm around her back and yanked his mouth away, his breathing labored. Her heart racing and her pulse thick and heavy, she turned her face against his neck, the warmth of his hand filling her with a heavy weakness.

"You feel so good," he whispered raggedly, dragging his fingers against her hardened nipple. Her whole body trembling, Tally turned her face tighter against the soft skin of his neck.

Freeing his hand from her top, he slid it under her hair to cup the back of her neck, holding her even closer. "There's not enough room on the sofa," he said unevenly, his touch meant to comfort as he stroked her skin. He took a deep breath, rubbing his hand up her neck, and then spoke again, a hint of amusement in his voice. "I have a perfectly good bed."

Not sure she was going to be able to stand on her own, Tally loosened her grip, but Christien didn't let go of her. Rising with her in his arms, he wasted little time moving them into his dark bedroom.

He released her just enough to let her slide down his body, groaning when any body part touched the hardness beneath his pants zipper.

Once her feet touched the floor, he slid both hands

up her rib cage and under her top. Drawing an un-steady breath, he eased away from her and watched intently as she moved her fingers up to the knot and released the halter top.

Christien went very still, his lips parted on a sharp intake of breath, making her feel feminine and sexy and completely wanton. She stood before him, let-ting him look his fill, purposefully drawing out the anticipation.

"Cup them for me, Tally. Lift them up."

Her nipples hardened immediately and she groaned softly, shocking herself at the heat that radi-ated off her skin when her palms curled under her breasts.

"You're beautiful," he said softly.

His hands went to her waist, as he drew her toward himself, she arched her back, thrusting her breasts out even more. When his hot, moist mouth tugged on her hard nipple, she felt a tugging, throbbing sen-sation in her clit.

He released her nipple to lave and torment the other tip, until Tally was gasping. Hooking his thumbs in the stretchy waistband of the skirt, he stripped the garment from her, jamming her breath in her chest.

His breathing ragged, he wrenched his shirt free of his pants and jerked it off in one movement. Tally weakly rested her head against his jaw, her whole body starting to unravel.

The instant he was free of his shirt, he roughly whispered her name and hauled her flush against him, and Tally lost a whole piece of reality when he rubbed his chest against her breasts. Catching a handful of hair, he brought her head back, covering her mouth with a kiss that was meant to incite, to ignite, to devastate. Adjusting the fit of his mouth against hers, he absorbed the sounds she made, running his hands up her rib cage, rolling her hardened nipples with his thumbs.

Tally couldn't stand it. Fighting for every breath against the frenzy inside her, she drank in the sweetness of his mouth, drawing his tongue deeper and deeper. Sobbing against his mouth, she fumbled to release the buckle on his belt, then ran her fingertips up the thick, hard ridge under his zipper and molded her hand against it.

Christien grabbed her wrist and yanked her hand away, making a hoarse sound deep in his throat. Bringing her arms around his neck, he tempered the kiss. Then he eased away from her and undid the front of his pants. His breathing harsh and labored, he rested his forehead against hers, as if collecting some control. His hands splayed wide on her hips, he slowly, slowly moved down her body.

Tally clutched his shoulders when he moved his hot, wet mouth across her belly. Straightening, he caught her in his arms and placed her onto the bed; before she had time to react, he had his pants off and was beside her.

Drawing air through clenched teeth, he dragged her against him, and Tally's senses went into overload when his body connected with hers, the feel of him thick and hard and fully aroused at the juncture of her thighs.

He quickly covered her mouth with another searing kiss, his fingers tangling in her hair, his heart hammering against his chest. Tightening his hold on her, he wedged his knee between her legs and then pressed her onto her back, and Tally fought for breath as he settled heavily between her thighs. The feel of him was wonderful. It was almost too much and, somehow, not enough.

He scooted downward and her world turned on its axis. Kneeling between her spread thighs, his lips drifted along her quivering belly. His breath was warm on her skin as he kissed and nuzzled his way lower, until he reached the barrier of silk and lace. He nipped playfully at the fabric, teasing her with the promise of something much more pleasurable.

"Take them off," she ordered, not at all shocked at hearing the demanding tone of her voice.

Giving in to her urging, he tucked his fingers into the waistband of her panties and slid them down her thighs and off, then repositioned her legs so they remained open, giving him an unobstructed view of the most intimate part of her.

He skinned out of his boxer-briefs and heat curled through her as she caught her first glimpse of his erection, so thick and huge. He reached for one of the foil packets in a side drawer, tore it open and rolled the condom down his straining shaft.

Then he sat back on his heels and his smoldering dark eyes took in every inch of her. Feeling naughty and daring, she lifted her hips and a frenzied light gleamed in his eyes. She brought her hands between her thighs, using her fingers to spread herself open, exposing her need for him in a way that should have made her feel vulnerable, but instead empowered her, because at the moment she felt like the one in control.

His strong hands, slightly rough and callused, pushed her legs wider apart to make room for the width of his shoulders as he settled in between.

His soft, dark hair tickled her skin as he lowered his head, the silky touch of his tongue both a relief and pure torment, wringing a husky moan from her.

He laved her in sleek strokes and she gasped when he put one long finger, then two, deep inside her, and then gradually withdrew them, only to sink back into her in a slow, languid thrust.

On the verge of spiraling apart, her body quaked with need and her inner muscles contracted. She heard herself whimper, arched into his skillful mouth and begged him to finally end the fierce, burning ache he'd stoked within her.

Accommodating her, he closed his mouth over her clit, tonguing and teasing that taut knot of nerves while his fingers continued to slide deep, deep inside her. He sucked harder and her fingers twisted in his hair as she came on a shuddering orgasm that seemed to go on and on and on. The pleasure that shot through her was sharp and riveting and left her breathless, but not satisfied.

He moved up and over her, the slide of his hard frame along the length of hers made her pulse leap higher and faster, as did the way he fit his lean hips between her still trembling thighs, which forced her legs high around his waist. He took control as easily as he made her gasp, pinned her beneath him so that he could have his wicked way with her.

His chest crushed her breasts as he braced his forearms on either side of her head, and his sheathed erection, so hot and eager, channeled along her sensitive flesh and found the soft, slick entrance to her body. Before she could recover from the aftershocks of her dizzying climax, he drove into her, high and hard and unexpectedly deep.

She sucked in a sharp breath at the abrupt sensation of being stretched and filled so completely. Her fingers curled around his biceps, her back arched and she cried out.

He met her gaze and brushed back the tendrils of hair lying against her cheek with a touch so gentle her chest tightened with a startling connection that seemed to transcend their physical joining.

"Finally inside you," he said.

That admission destroyed her defenses in a way she'd never anticipated—a scary prospect when this night with him should have been all about sex and pleasure—nothing more. And while she'd undoubtedly experienced both in varying degrees, she told herself that she couldn't afford to form an emotional attachment to this man, not when her life was ready to even out.

"Are you going to talk or are you going to move? Please say you're going to move those hips."

He withdrew and surged forward with a quick movement of his hips, then he slowed, thrusting hard and deep when he was to the hilt inside her. He groaned, the sexy masculine sound reverberating against her chest and belly.

"You feel so good," he rasped.

"So do you." Smoothing her flattened hands down the sinewy slope of his spine, she palmed his taut buttocks, which flexed as he pulled back and then glided to the hilt once again.

"Don't stop," she said hoarsely, feeling that gradual steady climb toward yet another climax.

"Never crossed my mind." His eyes blazed hotly, and the smile that curved his lips was a heady combination of seductive intent and primal desire.

She managed a laugh that turned into a breathy moan when he rotated his pelvis against her, generating a stimulating pressure that was as possessive as it was arousing.

Wrapping her legs tightly around his waist, she urged him to a faster rhythm.

Thrusting in her, he gave her what he'd promised, increasing the pace and riding her with a wild, fierce aggression. Capturing her lips with his, he kissed her, his mouth and tongue just as demanding and as insistent as the way he was claiming her body.

His thrusts grew stronger, deeper, harder. His hips urged her into lifting her own, meeting his in an uncontrollable response as he powerfully buried himself in her, over and over, until her orgasm crested in a fiery rush of pleasure. Her release was so intense, so all consuming, she wrenched her mouth from his and screamed, *"Christien,"* losing herself utterly in him and the exquisite sensations.

He was right there with her, tossing his head back with a low, feral growl, his hips grinding against hers as his own climax rumbled through him. After one last shuddering thrust, he slumped against her and buried his face in the crook of her neck, seemingly trying to gather his equilibrium, which she completely understood because she was struggling to do the same.

Finally, he lifted his head and gazed down at her, the slow grin spreading across his face drowsy and full of male satisfaction. *"Dieu,* Addison, you are good in bed."

She smiled right back at him. The man was too irresistible. She could feel her defenses being breached, but couldn't seem to stop her common sense from crumbling. "You're no slouch, yourself, sugar. Nice. Really, really nice."

He reached up and opened the window over the bed. The crack was enough to cool the room slightly, but not cold enough to make them shiver.

"Do you sleep with the window open a lot?"

"Not here in New Orleans, but I did when I lived in Bayou Gravois."

She could hear the longing in his voice and Tally wondered how it would be to have such a connection to a place that the love for it was audible just in the sound of your voice. "You miss it?"

"Yes, I do. I get back when I can. I'd love to take you there some day."

"Take me there now. I want to see it through your eyes first, Christien."

His face softened, his eyes unfocusing as he slipped into the past. In a deep, seductive voice, he said, "I guess dawn would have to be the best time for me. My dad used to take me crayfishing. We'd maneuver our pirogue out into the bayou, travel for about an hour in the predawn light, crisscross a maze of waterways, cut through dense curtains of willows and hardwood trees with clinging, tattered moss.

"We didn't talk. We'd just listen to the song of the bayou. Gulls flocked in the air as my dad dipped his paddle into the thick, muddy water. Dawn crept silently up into the trees. Through the misty air, the reddish earth and the gray-green country looked like a dreamscape.

"So many different trees—cypress, sweet gum, persimmon and water locust. Their branches and leaves mingled in a living canopy overhead.

"As we moved deeper into the bayou, it's as if the world slipped away. The place renewed my body and spirit. Maybe what people say about the swamps is true—it's full of magic."

"It sounds so beautiful."

"You've never been out in the bayou?"

"No, I've always been a bit afraid of the water snakes and the alligators."

"Ah, no, *chère*. All part of the wild beauty of the bayou. They belong there and we visit. Little ole gators won't bother you. As long as you respect them, they'll respect you."

"I have a full and lingering respect for *little ole gators,* thank you very much. But I have to say that the picture you paint is beautiful, something I would love to experience with you, Christien."

"Then we will, Tally. I promise."

A breeze blew across her heated skin and her nipples puckered. Very gently, he trailed his fingertip from her cheekbone all the way to the hard tip of her nipple.

"So far, you've made me scream out your name. How about I get to experience my other fantasy?"

"Which one would that be?"

"Running my mouth and my hands all over you."

"Okay, but only for about a hundred years. Then you'll have to stop."

Lifting herself up, she slipped her pelvis over his hips.

"You want to do it from that vantage point, huh?"

"Yes, I want to watch your face." She gasped as

his cock lengthened and hardened beneath her. "Oh, hey, didn't you say something about riding a guy won't get me the results I want? Hmmm. It seems you were wrong about that."

"I'm very glad to be wrong."

Christien chuckled and tried to reach out for her, but she grasped his wrists and pulled them over his head, trailing her hands down the soft skin on the inside of his wrist and over his forearms and rock-hard biceps. "Oh, please, keep those wonderful hands to themselves. I don't want to be distracted."

She smoothed her palms over his shoulders, down his taut pectoral muscles, the heated velvet of his skin tingling against hers.

She pressed her clit to his scorching cock, which did absolutely nothing to relieve the insistent ache and throbbing in her pelvis. "Touching you like this is getting me so very wet, Christien."

He made a deep sound in his throat. Leaning down, she flicked her tongue over the flat disk of his nipple and his hips surged off the bed. "Oooh, sensitive there. That's hot, soooo…" she flicked him again "…very…" once again just to feel him thrash and hear that delicious sound of surrender from him again "…hot." She did it again and he twisted under her mouth, his groan rumbling in his chest. Closing her lips over that bead, she sucked him hard.

"What would it feel like to have my mouth around your cock like this, Christien?"

"Vous êtes massacre je," he said, translated into, "You're killing me."

"Ah, j'ai seulement commencé." Tally said, telling him she was just beginning her exploration.

"You're going to make me come if you keep talking to me like that."

"Oh, that won't do," she said softly, trailing her lips down his rippled abdomen, kissing each heated ridge, each satiny valley. The closer she moved toward his groin, the more restless he became. Slipping her hand around his thick shaft, she tightened her fist. "Tell me what you want, sugar."

"Take my cock in your mouth and suck me," he demanded.

She did as he asked, causing his hips to roll and a guttural moan to issue from his mouth. She swirled her tongue over the plump, sensitive crown of his cock, pulling him into her mouth, all the way to the base of his shaft. She sucked him hard and strong, leading him to the brink of ecstasy, and then pushed him over the edge into a frenzied rush of satisfaction.

He growled her name, his entire body shuddering as he came in a long, thick stream, his climax so all-consuming and powerful that it left him gasping for breath.

Tally was throbbing, her clit full and engorged. Reaching down, she had to relieve herself, but Christien rose up and slipped his hands under her arms, dragging her up his body. "Come here, *bruja,* and ride my mouth."

"Calling me a witch, are you?" she gasped. Her hot, dazed eyes going over that delectable mouth, the soft lips ready to give her body the release it was clamoring for.

She eased herself forward and straddled his head, giving him open contact to her engorged sex. She braced her hands on the small windowsill in front of her to steady herself.

She whimpered as he nuzzled and kissed the inside of her thigh, called out when his breath gusted over her wet, swollen flesh and, when he finally tasted her with a slow, intentional lick, she screamed his name for the second time as he swirled his tongue around her clit and gave her body what it ultimately craved.

His fingers tightened around her thighs, holding her while he took her greedily with his mouth. His tongue was hot and aggressive, ruthless and demanding, unfurling deep and stroking and suckling with insatiable hunger. Another thrust of his tongue, and a lusty moan ripped from her as she climaxed in wild, exquisite abandon.

He didn't let her go right away. He lapped at her more slowly now, drawing out her pleasure, forcing her to endure, to ride out her release until the last small spasms jerked through her spent body, only then did he take his hands from her thighs, and she slid down to his side.

Snuggling into the crook of his arm, she closed her eyes, melting instantly into tears. Words deserted her. There was only twisted-up raw emotion. It was enough for her just to touch him, feel his body fitting against hers, to stare into his eyes. Two halves of a prefect whole. The wonder of it made her tremble.

She could not help giving him what he needed. She wanted to heal all his wounds, fulfill all his dreams—too bad she just didn't believe in them.

TALLY JERKED OUT of a nightmare, one full of hazy terrors and the unknown, words whispered in her brain. *He's going to ruin everything. He's going to break a heart you can't afford to have broken again. It was smart to keep it free of entanglements. Ambition is all that you need. It'll sustain you.*

She looked at his solemn face and her heart melted. He was relaxed in sleep, but still that raw male magnetism radiated around him. His hair lay in tangled disarray, dark and rich against the white bed linens, a lone strand across his cheek. She reached out and captured it, her fingers rasping against the five o'clock shadow outlining his strong jaw, and rubbed the silky strand between her thumb and forefinger.

His broad shoulders took up a lot of space. Her eyes trailed to his rock-solid chest, his taut stomach bare to the night and her prying eyes.

She released the strand and backed out of bed being as quiet as possible so as not to wake him. Finding her clothes in the dark, she dressed, her heart pounding, her heart telling her to get back into that bed and her head yelling at her to get out and go home where she could think more clearly.

Determined to leave before her emotions got any more tangled up in this brief fling, she wheeled toward the door, but stopped and turned back. Biting her lip in indecision, she trembled in the room. Backing away, she broke that mesmerizing hold he had on her and slipped out of his bedroom and his apartment. With her keys in hand, she headed to her car.

Despite looking for an unforgettable sexual encounter, she feared she'd gotten way more than she'd bargained for with Christien Castille.

On her way home, Tally passed the Count's quiet piazza. The gaping hole where the tree had been made her feel even more melancholy.

Tally let herself into her town house, her heart

aching already. She was walking toward the kitchen light switch when she hit a solid barrier of cold that chilled her to the core. Her heart climbed into her throat and she stumbled backward. Light illuminated the room in a blinding flash. A man stood before her, but he wasn't dressed in modern clothes.

Her jaw dropped at the solidness of his presence, making the hair on her whole body rise as if charged by what felt like electricity filling the room.

"I understand you're looking for my treasure," the apparition said.

Tally retreated quickly, her heel catching on the carpet, landing her soundly on her backside.

7

A SOUND WOKE HIM AND EVEN before Christien was aware of that soft noise, he instinctively knew that Tally was gone. The sheets were still warm from her body heat. The other evidence that she'd even been in his bed were the tangled covers and the scent of sex.

Glancing at the digital display on his clock radio, Christien saw that it was just past five.

He rolled to his back, scrubbed a hand over the stubble on his jaw and cursed vividly.

Tally was making a statement here, one he wasn't too dense to understand. She wanted a fling. Nothing more. Yet she'd asked him some pretty personal questions and her interest in him hadn't been an act. Tally was a myriad of contradictions. Though, simply put, he wanted her to want more with him.

He wasn't moved at all by the female attention he'd gotten in the Spirit of Fluxus last night. Part of the reason had to do with the fact that he was working, but the biggest part had to do with Tally.

From the moment he'd seen her wheeling around the tables at Café Eros, he'd been intrigued by her mixture of sweetness and sass. In the past, he'd have been grateful for a woman to spare him the awkward after-sex morning by hightailing it out of his apartment in the middle of the night.

But not today. Today he had half a mind to get up, go over to her town house. He'd wanted to savor waking up with her, making breakfast for her, and having some time to connect before he started another day.

But he also knew that getting into someone's face wasn't going to get him what he wanted. Tally was independent. The harsh realities of her early life had fashioned Tally into the woman she was today.

There were no easy answers, just a voice in his head that told him that Tally was worth his time and effort. Whatever was between them had the potential of developing into something stronger and bigger than the both of them if nurtured slowly and carefully— with a little bit of romance and a whole lot of trust.

No problem on the romance-and-trust front. But the patience that going slowly required, well, his track record didn't bode well for his success in that department.

He threw off the covers and grabbed for a pair of jeans.

Before his hand closed over the denim, his cell phone rang.

Christien searched for the phone. "Castille," he said when he'd finally flipped the phone open!

"Christien, our boy is on the prowl," his former colleague said.

"Where?"

"Meet me in the Garden District at Vine and Plantation."

"I'll be there in ten minutes."

After throwing on clothes, Christien jumped into the seat of his car. Dropping his cell phone into the pocket of his leather jacket, he thought he should talk to Tally about where they were headed.

He couldn't remember being this edgy or pumped up over a woman before, but with his sick sense of humor, it served him right and he was kinda turned on by it. Pursuing someone who was so worth the heartache that could be waiting for him at the end of it all stirred his blood in a way that he hadn't ever experienced before. It made him feel alive and vibrant, as if he could take on the world and win.

He loved living in the French Quarter except in the high tourist season. He took Canal to St. Charles and was soon in the Garden District.

Jim Carter pushed away from his parked car

when Christien pulled up. They greeted each other with a handshake.

"What's up?" Christien asked.

Jim gestured toward the majestic house in front of him. "He was casing the place."

"He's finally making a move?"

"Looks like it. He's been waiting six months, but the compulsion to steal again must be taking its toll," Jim said, leaning against the car once again.

"He still has no idea we're keeping tabs on him."

"No. He doesn't seem to have a clue."

"You'll check out the owners tomorrow and let me know what you find out?" Christien asked.

"Of course."

"I bet there's an older woman living there."

Jim gave his friend a sly look and rolled his eyes. "I don't take sucker bets."

"Thanks for staying on him. I know it plays havoc with your personal life, Jim."

"Christien, when are you going to stop being a jackass and get back on the force?"

"I'm not coming back."

"Don't lie to me. I know you love the job."

"Is that your way of telling me you miss me, Carter?"

"Screw off, Castille. I'll call you tomorrow with the particulars."

Christien got in his car and headed back to his apartment—maybe he could catch a couple more hours of sleep.

TALLY SAT ON THE FLOOR looking up at Captain Gabriel Dampier in the…er… Oh God, it was his actual ghost.

"Speak up, girl. Come now, you cannot possibly be surprised. You have seen me and heard me before."

She had. It was true, but having him stand in front of her and address her was a bit disconcerting to say the least. Surely, he had to give her a moment to take it all in.

His attire was vastly different from what he wore in the mural on the Café Eros wall. He appeared in a pair of fawn breeches and black knee-high boots; Hessians, Tally was sure they were called. The white billowing shirt with lace at the cuffs and the crimson long coat were all pirate. Captain Dampier was extremely attractive for a dead guy; the mural and all the paintings she had stored in the attic didn't do him justice.

The gray eyes that regarded her were as deep and subtle as smoke from a wildfire. The face exquisitely male and finely formed; a cool sulky mouth, an aquiline profile; and a sure intelligence in the assessing look he gave her. The harsh light behind him lit a smoldering halo of reddish-gold around his black hair.

She swallowed hard and swallowed again. She had his features. Why had she never seen it in the paintings and the mural? How had she not seen that she and Bree carried the exotic Mediterranean French ancestry in their very genes, genes shared with this man?

He was their beginning, the man who'd formed their line and was responsible for her very existence; and, against her will, she felt a...connection that had existed long before she had seen or heard him. She'd only become aware of it just now.

He braced his hands on his thighs and gazed down at her.

Trembling inside from either excitement or terror, she couldn't be sure, she straightened her shoulders, attempting at least the image of composure.

Tally pushed up from the floor and gave in to her curiosity. She reached out, but her hand went right through him. "You look so real."

He smiled. "Alas, I am not."

"I feel like I should offer you something to drink."

"Aye, good ale would go down nicely. But it would be a waste. I would not taste a thing."

"Too bad," Tally said, moving into the living room

on shaky legs. She needed to sit down before she fell down again.

"It is. But getting landlocked in Court du Chaud was a tangle of my own making." He followed her into the room. There was an efficient grace to his movement, a swing and balance that seemed to assess the ground beneath him, to interpret and exploit terrain instead of merely walk upon it, like the innate ability of a man who sailed through storm-tossed seas and rolling waves.

"Are you talking about the curse you're under?" she asked as he made a gesture and the bench slid away from the piano all by itself. He settled on the polished wood.

"Yes, indeed, the deuced curse. How do you know about that?"

Tally closed her gaping mouth and swallowed hard. "My uncle told me."

"And he came by the information how?"

"Passed down through the generations of our family. All your descendants knew about the curse."

"And about the treasure. Tell me what you have done to secure it."

"You don't mind that I'm looking for it?"

"No. I led you to the journal, did I not?" He spread his arms. "Besides, what am I going to do with it? It's fitting that one of my descendants should possess it. How much progress have you made? Tell me, girl."

"None, actually, but now that you're here, you can just tell me where it is."

"I cannot do that for I do not recollect where I hid it. It's been two hundred years after all. Where is the map?" He frowned at her as if she were a navigational chart that had proved to be grossly inaccurate. "Explain this folly."

"My brother took it. He's disappeared and won't return my phone calls."

"Does he know what he possesses?"

"No."

"What steps have you taken to secure the missing map?"

"I've hired a private detective two days ago."

"Private detective?" He looked at her with a puzzled frown.

"A private detective takes money to find missing people."

"A mercenary, then?"

A knock sounded on her door. The captain seemed quite unconcerned.

"There is someone at the door."

"Then you'd better answer."

She hesitated.

"I'm not a figment of your imagination. I will wait to speak with you."

Tally opened the door to Christien. He stood on her porch with his shoulder propped against the side of the door frame, all arrogant, self-assured male, as if he had every right to be there. His thick, midnight hair was loose as if he hadn't wanted to take the time to pull it back; dark stubble lined his jaw and his brown eyes bore into hers. "What are you doing here?"

"I woke up to find you gone. Since it was my intention to share breakfast with you, I guess I'll have to do it here. You missed getting it in bed, though."

"I already got what I wanted in your bed, Christien."

He crowded her against the foyer wall and laughed. "Too bad, *chère*. I wasn't quite done with you yet."

Taunting amusement flickered across his features masking a look in his eyes that faded too quickly—hurt? Instantly, her hand came out and smoothed through his loose hair. She was surprised to find her hand trembling. There was so much more to this man than she had first realized.

He was a threat to everything she strived for, yet in the short amount of time she'd spent with him, she had experienced something more real than anything she'd ever hoped or imagined would be possible.

She couldn't turn him away, although she realized that she should. She could effectively end it here and now with a few words, but when she spoke, her words came from her heart. "Come in and we'll have some breakfast. I don't have to be to work until the lunch shift."

He walked toward the kitchen and Tally followed. When she glanced toward the piano bench, she did a double take. The captain hadn't moved. He grinned and raised his brows.

"I'm really hungry," she said, thinking to keep Christien busy so she could get rid of the captain.

"Do you have Tabasco?" Christien asked. Rolling up his sleeves to reveal his hard forearms, he looked at her expectantly.

"Yes," she said, turning away from the captain. She went to the refrigerator door, Christien close on her heels. Reaching for the half-empty bottle in the door slot, she pulled it out and heard, "Is this the mercenary?"

She jerked at the sound. The captain materialized right next to her. The Tabasco bottle slipped out of her grasp and fell, hitting the floor right near where Christien stood.

"Damn," she said, biting her lip.

Christien said. "Now my raging Cajun eggs won't be the same."

She glared at the captain but the sparkle in his eyes told her he was having fun.

With a soft exclamation, she took a step towards the mess.

"Don't," Christien said. "I'll clean it up."

She felt the small act of kindness down to her toes. No one except her sister had ever seemed to care.

"Trying to be my hero?"

He smiled at her: a sleepy, warm smile, his eyes a tangled brush of dark lashes and ebony heat. "Maybe."

He watched her for a moment, his gaze moving to her mouth and shoulders with raking leisure.

"Good, because I don't need one, Christien." She stepped inside, but he blocked her from escaping.

"Ah, Tally. Everyone needs a hero. It's too bad there aren't enough to go around."

The captain showed no signs of fading away. He watched them avidly, as if his very existence hinged on what he would see. Only a foot separated her from Christien. She felt the heat radiating from him, but yearned for him to move closer. His breath fanned her face with a light, sensuous touch.

"I don't believe in fairy tales and happily-ever-after, either," Tally stated.

The captain frowned and shook his head, but Christien nodded his. "A practical, hard-edged modern woman."

"I do have sharp edges, Christien. Be careful you don't get cut."

"I'm tough, Tally."

Why did that look in his eyes break her heart—a weary, disillusioned look that caused a lump in her throat. Unexpected feelings, unwanted intimacy. Yet, she couldn't help reacting to those dark eyes, from falling into his sea of pain. Something she was sure he'd hidden well over the years.

"You have to be in this world, Christien. You have to be. Nothing is ever perfect."

"No, it's not, except how you feel in my arms."

She shook her head. "No, nothing." The only real thing in life was cold hard cash and the promise of the comfort and safety it could buy.

Pragmatic, tough-minded as she was, she couldn't explain why her heart melted, why a need rose in her to reach out, touch him, as if simple human contact could make anything better.

His chin dropped as her hands reached out to cup his head, his hair like silk against the sensitive pads of her fingers. Fire licked her insides as she lifted his face to her searching eyes.

"Let me see what I can do about that toughness," she whispered. "Make you burn."

He pulled her hips against his, his groin fitting into the notch like he was made for her.

Transfixed, she watched silently as his gaze traveled down her length, then slowly began the journey back up, lingering on her breasts until her nipples hardened. When he lifted his head there was a knowing look in his eyes.

He closed the distance, his breath tickling her ear when he whispered, "I'm Cajun...so it's going to have to be damned hot to burn me."

Turning slightly until her lips grazed his ear, she said, "From the inside out, Christien." She felt the shudder sweep over him. "Like fire under your skin, like a fever." Her voice low and husky. "There are ways to orgasm that would blow your mind."

"Give me fever."

She closed her eyes at the underlying dare in his words.

When she opened them, she saw the captain standing with his arms across his chest. Caught up in the seduction of Christien, she'd totally forgotten the ghost was there. She snapped out of Christien's arms and almost fell, saved only by Christien's lightning-quick move as he grabbed hold of her shoulders.

"What the hell?" he asked confusion thick in his deep voice.

Tally stared at the captain.

"Is this your mercenary?"

"He's not a mercenary."

"What?" Christien asked, still clearly confused.

"I can see now that this man is much more than a mercenary," the captain said. "Is he your lover?"

"That's none of your business," she hissed under her breath. "Be quiet, he'll hear you."

"Tally, he can't hear me or see me."

"You left that joy for me alone," she asked sarcastically.

"Tally, what are you muttering?" Christien moved to stand next to her. Tally gave a quelling look to the captain and jerked her head toward the stairs.

"Do you mind if I run upstairs and take a quick shower?" Tally said inching toward the polished cypress stairs.

Christien shook his head. "I'll start the eggs."

"I have another bottle of Tabasco up in the cabinet. I really want a taste of those…er…raging Cajun eggs."

"Great." Looking bewildered, he rounded the counter and entered the kitchen.

Tally laughed nervously, giving Christien a sheepish smile. She turned her back on him and mouthed to the captain. "Upstairs."

Once she was safely in her bathroom with the captain, she said, "If you're going to haunt my house, then we're going to have some ground rules."

"Ground rules?"

"Rules that indicate how you'll behave while there is another person in the house."

"What rules do you wish me to follow?"

"When Christien is here, what happens between us is private. You—" she shoved her finger at him "—disappear, and I mean that literally."

"But it's very interesting to watch you try to resist the…er…raging Cajun."

"After two hundred years, all you have is jokes?"

"It is good to be amused after all this time."

"Agree, or you can go haunt someplace else."

"Agreed. What else?"

"You don't watch me in my bedroom, do you?"

His eyes flashed in an odd way that made Tally remember this was a ghost and not an ordinary man.

He raised his chin and said, "No! What kind of a cad do you take me for? The very idea. I am a gentleman, not a Peeping Tom."

Tally leaned against the wall, suddenly exhausted with what she'd been through, first with Christien and now Captain Dampier's very real, very indignant ghost. "That's a relief."

"Now you tell me something, Tally."

"What?"

"Why do you collect what was once mine?"

"Someday it will fill a Captain Dampier wing of a museum."

He blinked at her as if the words she'd uttered had been a foreign language. He looked down and away, then back at her, still speechless. She watched his face. It held distance. Time and space...and memories. He swallowed. "That is quite...remarkable."

"Why? You helped save New Orleans along with Lafitte, but he got all the glory."

His brows furrowed as if confused about her motivation. "He was a great strategist."

She held his eyes, keeping her chin steady. "I'm not trying to take anything away from Lafitte. He was a dashing figure, but he made his own mark in a town that scorned him."

"Are you saying that I did not?"

"No, you didn't. You faded into obscurity."

His jaw set moodily, his features grim and dark above the scarlet long coat, he said, "I died in my prime."

"I want to set history straight and you deserve your place in it."

"This is so very unexpected. I thought with the treasure…"

The ache in his voice made her throat close. He'd been alone with his curse and the reality of his death, trapped in Court du Chaud for all time. "The treasure is a separate issue."

"But you don't have to do anything for me, Tally. That's not warranted. The crone was very wrong about you."

She wanted to ask who the crone was, but the captain spoke before she could utter a word.

"This is an act of kindness I did not believe could come from one of my descendents after all the heartache I caused for the one I held so very dear."

"It's the right thing to do, Captain."

"Tally?" The deep sound of Christien's voice made her heart beat faster.

The captain looked at her for a moment, then said, "Please address me as Gabriel," before he simply dissolved then disappeared.

8

CHRISTIEN KNOCKED AGAIN. When he got no response, he called out. "Tally?"

He thought he heard her voice.

The door opened and Tally stood before him still fully dressed.

"Who were you talking to in here?"

"I was singing in the shower."

He looked at the glass-enclosed shower and cocked his eyebrow. "Tally, the shower isn't even on."

She turned to look, then faced him with a sheepish smile. "I got a head start."

Walking over to the shower stall, she flipped the gleaming knobs and turned on the water, adjusting it as it got hot. She'd been acting strangely since the Tabasco sauce incident.

"The eggs are ready."

She turned to look at him.

"What have you been doing all this time?"

Her eyes raked his frame in a caress that felt almost physical, lingering at his groin. She raised her eyes to his, a suggestive smile on her lips.

Just far enough away, she pulled her shirt over her head and dropped it to the floor. Next, she reached behind her back to unhook her bra. As soon as the catch came undone, her breasts spilled free, lush and voluptuous, the tight points of her nipples jutting toward him as if begging for his touch.

"Thinking about you."

She tossed off her shoes, then unzipped her jeans and shimmied them over her hips, down her thighs, and off her long, slender legs, leaving her wearing nothing more than a pair of bikini panties and a come-and-get-me smile that nearly undid him. He waited for her to remove that last scrap of fabric so he could look his fill of her, but she had something else in mind.

He had a vague thought that she was deliberately distracting him, but at the moment he couldn't seem to put two words together to form a thought, let alone put a coherent sentence together.

Holding his gaze, she walked up to him. Flattening her hand in the center of his chest, she skimmed her cool palm downward, her fingers dragging over his ribs and taut abdomen. She didn't stop there, and he gave a raw moan of pleasure as her fingers curled along the thick length of his erection confined behind denim.

His body jerked in response when she stroked him. It was all he could do not to take her right there on the bathroom floor.

Without preamble, she licked her lips and put her mouth over his nipple. He felt the incredible tugging, pulling sensation all the way to his cock. He couldn't stop the long, low groan that seemed to come from the depths of him. He rocked his pelvis against hers, his body tense and quivering.

Her sensual gaze lifted to his, and the smile that etched her expression was a combination of exhilaration and pure bliss, as if she were under the influence of a very potent aphrodisiac.

"I can't get enough of that, *chère*."

She leaned forward, ran her lips over a taut pectoral muscle, and then took a soft, ravenous bite from his flesh. She groaned against his skin; a hot wild tremor rippled through him in response.

"You taste delicious, much better than eggs, raging or otherwise." She pressed her cheek against his chest, rubbing against him like a cat. "So warm and wonderful."

She palmed his erection, stroking his cock from the base all the way up to the engorged tip. She turned her head to look at him, her skin flushed pink, her expression reflecting erotic pleasure, and her soft brown eyes feverish with a desperate need for him.

She wrapped her arms around his neck and brought his mouth down to hers. The pressure of her mouth parted his lips and her tongue slipped inside to tangle with his. Her fingers threaded through the hair at the nape of his neck, her breasts crushed against his chest, and the carnal mating of their mouths generated enough heat to make them both combust.

Her hand moved from around his neck down to the belt of his jeans. Working the leather loose, unfastening the snap of his jeans, she carefully lowered the zipper over his burgeoning shaft.

Grasping the waistband of his jeans and briefs, she pulled both downward and stopped once she pushed everything below his thighs.

"Oh my," she breathed.

He automatically thought she was talking about his stiff erection, but he looked down to see that she was thoroughly transfixed by the tattoo of a band of flames that streaked across his thick quadricep muscle and ended at the back of his thigh.

"I didn't get a good look at this before. Most people wear these around their arms."

"I like to be different."

She leaned forward and put her lips on the tattoo.

Christien sucked in a quick breath; the spiraling sensation of her soft mouth sent a message directly to his already hard, raging cock.

"And I didn't think you could turn me on any more." She pushed the jeans and briefs off of him and brought him to the now-steamy shower.

Christien made no move to initiate anything as it was obvious to him that Tally wanted to explore his body. Through the steamy mist, her heavy-lidded eyes caught his, her coffee hair now a darker shade as a result of the hot water pouring from the spout overhead.

"Touch all you want. I remember quite vividly you said you wanted to run your hands all over me."

"Oh, yes." Reaching for the body wash on the side of the stall, she lathered her hands. She trailed her fingers up his muscular arms, around his biceps before continuing along his broad shoulders and down his muscled chest.

It was beyond him to hold back any longer. He savored her sweet feminine curves with his hands even as she brushed her fingertips along his body, so gently, so eloquently. She felt deliciously feminine.

Her caresses were slow and languorous as she smoothed the fragrant lather down his legs, lingering on the flame tattoo, tracing it to the sensitive skin of his inner thigh.

"Did it hurt when they used the needle there?"

"Like a bitch."

"I'll kiss it later," she promised with a sexier-than-sin smile. "You have a beautiful form."

"I'd rather look at yours."

She chuckled as she came up his other leg, smoothing the soap along his belly and around to his buttocks. He groaned when her stomach rubbed up against his arousal.

He braced his flattened palms on the tiled wall for support as she applied a skillful pressure to the taut tendons running along his shoulders, and he moaned in pleasure as her talented hands kneaded knotted muscles.

"You feel really tight, Christien," she murmured, using her thumbs to loosen the tension along his nape. "Are you working too hard, sugar? Or worrying too hard?"

Christien moaned at the relief as her firm fingers kneaded his skin, breaking up the knots between his shoulder blades. "Probably a little of both. I'm sure your muscles tell the same tale."

"I have my stresses. Nothing a good soak, candles and a glass of wine can't remedy," she responded, her fingers working their magic down the muscles bisecting his spine, her firm touch spreading goose bumps along his flesh.

He closed his eyes, shivering as her palms slid over his hips and her small hands curved up his chest to brush over and massage his aching nipples.

"When you find Mark, I'll have less to worry about," she said.

She leaned against him, her breasts a wet sensual goad, her taut nipples pebbling against his skin. She rested there as the water sluiced over them. He turned around and grabbed the body wash, soaping his hands. She gasped as he ran his hands over her breasts and down her stomach.

She closed her eyes as his palms slipped over her hips and his hands squeezed her bottom.

"Do you trust me?" he murmured.

Her eyes popped open and her deep brown eyes widened a bit. "I do. I trust you."

He easily nudged her feet farther apart and slipped his fingers along the crevice between her legs, teasing the swollen lips of her sex before retreating again.

She moaned as he used his thumb against her clit. He readjusted the shower head so the water poured along her back. He chased the soapy suds down her spine with his palms, leaving her skin satiny soft from head to toe.

She gasped as his parted lips skimmed the side of her throat and his tongue licked the moisture beading on her skin. Her nipples puckered.

She slanted her head to the side, giving him better access to her neck as the water sprayed over them.

Moving behind her, he pressed on her back until her hands were braced against the tiled wall and she was bent at the waist.

"Damn, you have a gorgeous ass," he said, pulling her against him so that her backside was pressed against his hard, hot cock. He nudged her legs open, crooking her knee.

"Christien," she pleaded.

"Tell me what you want," he said.

She pressed herself against his bold caress. Nuzzling her ear, he pulled her earlobe between his teeth and nipped it. "Tell me." His voice challenged her, soft and taunting.

He pushed her thighs apart and slid his finger inside her. Her hips rocked and she released a moan. He slid his hand out and thrust again, with two fingers, deeper.

His own hips thrust forward when she clenched around his fingers. His fingers slipped tenderly along the delicate folds of her sex, his other hand cupping her breast and tweaking the nipple, making her cry out.

"Christien, please stop fooling around."

She knew he grinned even though she couldn't see him. "If this is fooling around, I'm never leaving this shower."

"Damn," she said softly on a puff of laughter. "You are a tease."

"I am, but in a good way, right?" He rolled a condom onto his shaft and slid his thumb tenderly around her clitoris. She moved against his hand, seeking more contact.

"Christien, put that hot cock inside me, now."

He nudged his thick shaft against her and Tally's breath flowed out of her. Pushing a little deeper, she pushed back against him. He flexed his hips, pushing deeper still, his breath ragged. "Will that do?"

She wiggled against him with an impatient gasp. "No."

"You want more? How do you want it? Deeper?"

"Deeper," she whispered.

His fingers curled around her hip. "Harder?"

She nodded, opening and reaching for him with every part of her. "Yes," she demanded emphatically. "Harder. Now, Christien."

He thrust deep, his body slapping against her backside, jerking a sharp cry out of her throat. "Like that?"

"Yes." She sought his rhythm and pressed back to meet him. With each stroke, she was more soft and wet.

He pulsed his hips against her, using controlled strength while his long fingers coaxed, caressed, undid her. Satisfaction spiraled inside him as she clutched at his cock with small tight spasms.

She arched and worked herself against him frantically. Christien fought the intensity of the explosion gathering in his gut. He followed his instincts, gathering speed and force and giving her exactly what she wanted. One final hard, relentless thrust and she hurtled, yelling into another orgasm.

The feel of her orgasm was too much for him, the sensations thundering through him almost too intense to call pleasure. He surged into her, tight and unbearably intimate, his arms locked around her as he finally let himself get lost in the cascade of hot bursting pleasure.

SQUEAKY CLEAN AND SATED, Tally smoothed foundation onto her face, taking in a deep sigh as she heard movement down in her kitchen. Christien had promised to make her more eggs, but it was too bad they didn't have time to savor them and each other in her bed.

She felt the urge to go running down the stairs and tell him everything about the treasure, the captain's ghost and why she really needed to find her brother. But Christien was temporary. When it was over, as it would be, she would still have her plans and her independence intact.

Christien was the kind of man who made a woman realize she could lean if she needed to and he wouldn't think any less of her. The trouble was Tally would think so much less of herself.

She'd been honest with him in the kitchen. She didn't need a hero.

Yet, the moment she thought about what had happened in the shower, the more she felt her resolve weaken. She wondered if she just let herself go...

"You'd be making a big mistake."

The whisper lingered in the air like the threatening hiss of a coiled deadly viper. The hair on the back of Tally's arms lifted. Cold crawled over her skin and seeped into her bones.

"Love will only bring you pain." Anger strummed through every carefully enunciated word.

Tally backed away from the mirror and turned towards the door, but it slammed shut. The lights in the bathroom flickered on and off. Drums started to sound and a shaky voice chanted.

"Ambition is the key to your happiness."

Tally tried the knob, but the door wouldn't open. She whirled to face the mirror. A vision, shadowy and insubstantial, floated there. The air was full of death and beneath it all, a citrus smell, cloyingly sweet. In the glass a face formed—the face of a very old woman, wrinkled like an apple too long left in the sun, her eyes a piercing blue, her hair as white as salt.

"The man will ruin everything."

Tally watched the mirror with a sense of dread pushing at the base of her throat and a strange, lethargic numbness dragging on her. Dreamlike. No, nightmarish. If she could believe this was a nightmare, then it wouldn't be real. A trick of the mind. She couldn't decide what would be better—to be alert and terrified with the reality of the situation, or to be stunned senseless and believe it was all a bad dream.

But she'd already been visited by one ghost today and recognized the silliness of the thought. She wasn't Scrooge and Christmas was over.

"I make the decisions about my own life," she said to the apparition.

"Ha, just like my granddaughter. Giving her heart to someone who doesn't deserve it. Remove him from your life."

"I do as I please."

A wind howled around the bathroom, tearing at Tally's robe, clawing through her hair like bony fingers, as frigid as a winter's kiss. The drum cadence intensified and the chanting turned into a shriek.

"This is just a warning!"

Tally covered her head. There was a great whooshing sound as if she were suddenly in a vortex, and then everything went quiet. The door flew open and a great splintering sound rent the air like ice shattering over a frigid lake.

When Tally removed her arms and looked again at the mirror, a giant crack split it from one end to the other.

WHEN TALLY CAME DOWN the stairs, she was met with a half-naked Christien whistling a jazzy tune while he shook drops of Tabasco sauce over the eggs. It was pretty obvious that he hadn't heard a thing. Not surprising, since he couldn't hear Dampier or see him when he'd been standing not more than a foot away. She hadn't been prepared for another ghost and the old woman was really quite angry with Tally's decision to date Christien. Too bad. Her life was her own and no one was going to tell her what to do.

With the incident pushed to the back of her mind, Tally gathered her hair together, her hands still trembling as she took the last few steps, and pulled it into a long ponytail. "Mmmmm, I think it's a good idea for guys to cook."

"You're looking at my butt," he said, turning around to give her a wink and a knowing grin.

Tally laughed softly, feeling a little catch in her chest at the audacity of this man she'd allowed into her hea…home.

She came around the counter and sidled up to him. "So, is this one of your father's recipes?"

"*Non.* This one is all mine."

He forked up a bite for her and blew softly on the steaming eggs, colored a smooth red.

"What else did you put in these?"

"Ah, Tabasco is the only ingredient I'll give you. See if you can guess the rest."

She took the bite into her mouth and rich fire burned her tongue, flaming hotter as she chewed. "Hmmm, cream."

"Yes, and…"

Tally let the flavors roll around on her tongue. "Pepper."

"That's an easy one."

"Give me a minute." He forked up another bite. "Yes, cayenne and something…I can't figure it out."

"Cinnamon."

"Yes, that's it. Delicious."

"Have a seat and get to chowing or you'll be late for work."

He dished up her eggs and set two slices of toast on her plate.

"Food is a way of life for Cajuns. Right?" Tally asked.

"It's very closely tied to our culture. When we settled here, we used what was around us. Most of the dishes we're famous for were born out of necessity."

"I'd be willing to bet money that Louisiana seduces its visitors the way clever women often find their way to men's hearts—via their stomachs. What else do you like to cook?"

"Gumbo. It's one of my favorite dishes."

"Every Cajun has his own idea about what makes a good gumbo. But everyone agrees that the key to a good gumbo is in the roux—that wonderful flour and oil combination."

"It's the base for many Cajun dishes. My brother and I call it Cajun napalm."

"What do you put in your gumbo?"

"The holy trinity of Louisiana cooking—celery, onion and green bell pepper. Cajuns don't need to fix what isn't broke."

Tally polished off the eggs, washing away some of the burn with the rest of her coffee. "What do you mean?"

"Antoine's has been serving Cajun food for 165 years, with only subtle changes to its menu."

"I see your point."

"I have a question for you. What are you going to do with all that stuff you have piled in your office? I tripped on a box coming out of your bedroom. You're exploding into the hall," Christien said.

"I'll have to put some of those boxes in the attic where I have stuff piled to the rafters. I told you I wanted to give the captain his due."

"Part of the museum exhibition?"

"Yes, if I could be sure of what was his and what wasn't. I've got a lot of cleaning and cataloguing to do."

"I can help you. I used to be pretty good with paperwork." He captured her chin and said, "You look beautiful all ready for work."

Tally smiled wistfully. "That's what Mark used to say before he went to school."

"Did he give you a hard time when he was younger?"

"Yes, he did, but nothing serious. Just teenage stuff. He was a good kid and a good student." She bit her lip, sighing softly.

"What?"

"I'm beginning to realize how little I know about my brother's life and how narrow-minded I've been."

"You want the best for your brother, that's understandable."

"You should hear him sing. He can compose and write songs that are so beautiful. I'll be singing one of them tonight at the Blue Note."

"I'll look forward to hearing it. You want your brother to go to school for music, right?"

"Yes."

"Best way to stop him from doing that is to push him into it."

"I'm beginning to realize that." It was clear to her that she'd hurt Mark with her criticism and her nagging. She cringed thinking about all the times she'd sucked the joy out of one of his stories about the band. He'd taken it, too. She'd never once praised him for holding down a job, being responsible. The knowledge weighed heavily on her heart. The fact that she'd only wanted the best for him seemed empty. She could have been much more open-minded and understanding while Mark found himself. She regretted that the last time she'd talked to her brother, she'd criticized him for something he loved doing.

His cell phone rang and Christien pulled it out of his pocket and answered.

He turned away while Tally picked up their plates and went to the sink, rinsing them under the tap, setting everything into the dishwasher.

"That was Jim. I've got to go meet with him," Christien explained.

"No problem."

As he neared, she could sense the power he exuded, could feel the eroticism of his hot stare as he watched her. Could feel her own body respond instinctively to that intense awareness of what was happening between them. By the time he stood next to her, she was breathless and battling the urge to rip off his clothes and have her way with him.

Summoning a bit of defiance to keep from giving into that urge, she lifted her chin and pinned him with a direct look. "It's time for you to go, sugar."

"Yes, it is."

Tally nodded.

A lazy, seductive grin curved his lips. "Can I get a kiss before I go or are you just going to tease me with that mouth?"

She tried to ignore that jump in her stomach.

"I think we both know the answer to that question," she replied.

He leaned in so close, his warm breath fanned her neck and his lips brushed the lobe of her ear. His damp tongue multiplied the shivery sensations tenfold, and he added in a rough wicked whisper, "I think we do."

Tally gave herself over to the delightful feel of Christien's questing mouth along her lips. He brought every nerve ending to life, to the point of dizzying torment.

Hard, masculine contours of his broad chest pushed against her sensitive breasts as he pinned her hips and thighs to the counter.

He deepened the kiss, voracious and hungry, and she answered, sliding her arms around his neck and holding him tight.

He broke the kiss and kept her close for a few minutes.

"I'll see you tonight, *chère*," he said, separating himself and turning to go.

"Tonight," Tally echoed.

As soon as the door closed behind him, Tally heard the eerie sound of drums. She rolled her shoulders and refused to let some old woman ghost get to her. "You can stop with the theatrics," Tally shouted, with more bravado than she felt, her voice echoing in the empty house.

The problem was the old woman's words made Tally want to strengthen her resolve against letting Christien any further into her heart.

WHEN TALLY APPROACHED the café, it looked as if it were already filled close to capacity. Perry Brazille fell into step with Tally. She was very gypsy-looking, with dark thick curly hair, and lived in number sixteen. Tally only knew her as a customer, one who loved Chloe's creole hot sausage po'boy sandwiches.

"Hi, Tally. I need coffee."

"And a po'boy?"

Perry grinned. "Oh no, you've got me pegged."

"Come on in."

"I need an injection of caffeine before I go to my aunt Della's shop to help her out."

"What kind of shop?"

"Metaphysical stuff, charms."

"Really. Does she have charms to ward off evil ghosts?"

"Sure. Do you need one?"

"It couldn't hurt."

Perry must have caught the undercurrents of Tally's nervousness because she took her aside and said, "You didn't answer my question, Tally."

"I think my place is haunted, okay? I need the charm."

Perry eyes filled with sympathy. "No problem. I'll write down the directions for you. There's a really good psychic there, Kachina Leaping Water."

"Sounds Native American."

"She's Choctaw."

"Thanks. Sorry to be so snappy."

"I guess evil ghosts give you the right," Perry said and shivered.

CHRISTIEN ENTERED THE PRECINCT for the first time in six months. The usual din of ringing phones, clattering keyboards and raised voices seemed as familiar to him as a well worn pair of jeans—jeans he'd discarded.

At reception, Christien picked up his visitor's badge, took some good-old-boy ribbing from the sergeant there and headed up to the robbery division.

Jim was on the phone but he motioned Christien

to sit at the desk across from him. The desk that had once belonged to him. It seemed like another lifetime as he planted his backside into the cushy chair, one he'd specifically ordered himself. On the desk in front of him was a file. Jim motioned to it and Christien opened up the file.

Inside were unsolved cases of robbery/murder over in Baton Rouge and Christien realized that the suspect they'd been trailing had been fishing in a different stream.

Jim hung up the phone. "Your hunch was right on the money. I pulled those today. That's our guy's MO."

Christien nodded, sorry he'd been right. "I knew the dirtbag couldn't control himself for weeks, let alone six months. How many?"

"Three. They may not all be his, but I bet at least two of them are."

"Does an older woman live at that house he cased?"

"Yes. I knew that was a sucker's bet."

Christien rubbed the back of his neck, reaching down to adjust a gun that was no longer on his hip, a badge that was no longer in his pocket.

"How does it feel being back in the driver's seat?"

"I'm a P.I., Jim."

"And that's a very admirable profession, but it's

more exciting to be on the front lines instead of behind them."

Christien snorted. "You're so full of it."

"All you have to do is apologize."

"I'd rather eat glass." Christien remembered the day he'd lost the case. The self-recrimination had been running through him, thick in his blood. Memories of his inability to name his mother's killer jumbled with the self-recrimination. He really didn't deserve to be a cop.

And this was no longer his desk.

"Chris…"

Christien decided it was time he let this go. He needed to attend to his real job, the one that paid the bills. "Look, Jim, you've got him in your sights, you make the collar."

"Christien, this is our bust. We worked on this case together—a lot—and we lost it. I know I want another crack at this guy."

"And you deserve it. I'm not a cop anymore. And I'm not coming back." Christien pushed away from the desk and rose. "I've got my own cases I need to get to."

"You're a cop down to your cells, man," Jim said.

Jim's words didn't penetrate. Christien knew the score. He'd screwed up in a major way and, as a result, a killer had been set free.

"Christien, don't throw your career away."

Christien turned. "That dirtbag wants a public apology. I'm not giving it to him. That leaves me out, since the brass won't reinstate me until I apologize."

If he stood here any longer, he was afraid all the pent-up frustration of the past few months would come spewing out in an ugly vitriol.

Gritting his teeth, guilt and anguish running through him, Christien said, "Get him, Jim, so he doesn't do this again. Make it stick this time."

"Christien."

"Let it go, Jim." Their gazes locked and his friend managed to convey both calm and sympathy in his eyes. Christien looked away.

"Good luck," Christien said as he turned and left, looking neither right nor left.

Badly shaken by the disturbing feelings Jim's words had evoked, Christien rested his forehead against the steering wheel.

He had never been good at facing ghosts because he had never wanted to look back—looking back meant dealing with all that fear and hurt and shame. Looking back made it seem that he was searching for forgiveness.

He didn't think that was possible.

Then or now.

9

AS SOON AS TALLY GOT off WORK, she pulled the paper Perry had given her out of the pocket of her jeans. Looking at it to get her bearings, she started off for the New Age shop. It was only early in the evening.

After walking for a few blocks, Tally passed the New Orleans Museum of History. Deciding to take a quick detour, she went inside and walked through many exhibits, one featuring Jean Lafitte. It would be the perfect place for an exhibit featuring Captain Dampier, maybe even combine it with the Lafitte one. On her way out, Tally picked up a brochure to read through later.

The French Quarter, only one half mile by three-quarters, bustled with activity around the clock. The old worldness of the second- and third-story terraces felt intimate to Tally as she walked down the narrow, crowded streets. Nothing in the oldest part of New Orleans was polished, shiny or new-looking; instead, it had a naughty charm.

She passed bars, nightclubs, adult shops, gift shops and restaurants dominating the neon-bathed street. Recorded music blared from the shops and clubs. New Orleans residents went about their daily lives among the tourists who came for the vibrant carnival atmosphere, unusual shopping and overall mystique.

Finally, she reached Perry's aunt's shop. Sugar Blues was printed on a big, round blue crystal that served as the shop's sign. It was a three-story building graced with two balconies facing Chartres Street. Tally went through the blue squeaky door into the bright interior.

Burning candles and a strong aroma of incense permeated the air. A sign on the wall offered palm, tarot and psychic readings. The walls were covered with shelves sporting teapots, cups and a large selection of fine teas.

On a nearby table were metaphysical items, esoteric books, rare crystals and handmade gifts. A glass case held many items of jewelry.

On other tables scattered around the shop, Tally browsed through polished stones, rune sets, essential oils, herbs and a variety of candle choices.

Her neighbor Perry moved through the beaded alcove at the back of the shop and smiled when she saw Tally. "You made it."

"I can't go back home until I have a charm, something to ward off evil."

"She's not evil," said a voice. "She's angry and vengeful, but not evil." When the owner of the voice came into view, Tally was taken aback. A woman in her late twenties stood before her. She was of medium height and weight, but she seemed to fill up the room, exuding a calmness that settled over Tally.

She seemed so young to have such a wise voice. With her dark, straight hair that flowed down to her waist, her elegant nose and the high cheekbones, Tally would have pegged her as full-blooded Native American, but her piercing blue eyes spoke of a mixed ancestry. Dressed in a black cotton blouse tucked into a colorful slim cotton skirt, this woman didn't look like any psychic Tally had ever seen. Perry's psychic friend? "Kachina Leaping Water, I presume?"

"I am and I can see that you are very much in need of help, but I am afraid that charm won't be effective."

Tally's heart sank. "Why not?"

"A saint medallion won't help. As I said, she's not evil."

"She cracked my mirror and spoke in a really scary voice."

"Theatrics, as I am sure you already suspect."

"Then another kind of charm that protects me against ghosts."

Kachina studied her with those intense blue eyes, eyes that seemed to glow from within. "Do you really want to ward off the other ghost? I think not."

"You're right I don't want to ward him off. I need to speak with him."

"Then, I'm afraid that I can't help you," Kachina said, her eyes full of regret.

"Please don't tell anyone about this. One 'crazy' person in our family is enough," blurted Tally.

"You're searching for something," Kachina said, approaching her. "May I?" she asked, reaching for Tally's hand, her colorful wooden bracelets clacking against each other.

Tally shifted, instantly uncomfortable. "I'd also rather not talk about that."

"Even if I have information that might help you?" Kachina replied, her hand suspended, waiting for Tally's permission.

"You do?" Tally had come here for help. She extended her hand toward Kachina.

Kachina took her hand in hers, her skin soft and warm. She pressed Tally's fingers open, gazing down at Tally's palm. "When it comes time for the choice, you'll have a difficult decision to make. Choose wisely because more than one life is at stake. Don't be afraid to make the right one."

"How can that information help me?"

Kachina folded Tally's fingers over her palm and squeezed. "You will understand at the right time."

Tally looked at her neighbor. "Thanks anyway for trying, Perry."

"I wish we could have done more, Tally."

"Perry, could you go back and finish up that inventory of crystals for me?"

"Sure, Kachina. Bye, Tally."

Tally turned to go, but Kachina Leaping Water took hold of her arm.

"Your mother's absence had nothing to do with you, Tally."

"What?" Tally said, surprised.

"Make peace with yourself. Forgive her and move on with your life."

"I am moving on."

"Sometimes we are very good at tricking ourselves into thinking things are true because we say they're so. Most of the time, they're not."

Tally extricated her hand from Kachina's and stepped back. "Look I've got to go."

Outside the shop, Tally took a deep breath and headed back toward her town house. A shiver shot down her spine and she threw a look over her shoulder only to see Kachina standing in the doorway.

TALLY KNOCKED ON BREE'S DOOR. When her sister called out to enter, Tally found her in the kitchen. "I need to borrow a dress for tonight."

Bree wiped her hands on a dish towel. "You singing at The Blue Note?"

Tally opened her sister's cookie jar and snagged a chocolate chip cookie. "Yes, can you help me out?" She tipped the jar to offer one to her sister.

Bree thought for a moment and grabbed for a cookie. Her eyes lit up. "I have the gold spangle that's got the right flair for the Blue Note."

Tally polished off her cookie. "The Prada-shoes dress. Perfect."

Bree led her sister up to her bedroom and went to her closet and took out the dress, bending down for the shoes.

"Wow, I forgot how gorgeous those shoes are."

"I saved up a long time for them. I wanted something really spectacular to go with this dress I made. I'm getting pretty good at sewing. This moonlighting with designer Toni Maxwell is paying off."

"Do you resent her?" The words came out of Tally's mouth before she could stop herself.

"Who? Toni?"

"Mom. Do you resent her for leaving us alone

without support? For leaving Mark. God, he was only fourteen."

"A little. I wonder if I would have followed through and become a lawyer."

"I don't resent her."

"What? Why?"

"I hate her."

Bree's eyes widened. "Tally, you can't mean that."

"She ruined everything, Bree. I had a full scholarship and I wanted my marketing degree very badly. I certainly didn't want to become a waitress and lounge singer."

The floodgates were finally open; Tally let everything pour out of her. "I want more, Bree. I've always wanted more. From the time I watched her throw good money after bad. I didn't want to end up like that. I vowed I wouldn't be broke and pathetic."

"Oh, Tally."

"She left us, Bree. Knowing what would happen, she left us without a word. Without notice. I can't forgive her for that."

Her sister dropped the shoes and the dress. Bree put her arms around Tally and hugged tight.

"It's doesn't matter. We still have each other. All of us."

"If Mark comes back," Tally whispered. "What if he doesn't come back?"

"He will. I'm sure of it."

"I wish I could believe that."

BACK INSIDE HER TOWN HOUSE, Tally finished dressing, put up her hair and applied her makeup wondering at the psychic's words. How could the woman know so much about her inner workings when Tally had missed what had been buried so deep in her heart?

Did she really hate her mother?

Even as she thought it, she knew it was true. She left her room and hurried down the stairs.

"Tally?"

The captain made a popping noise as he appeared in front of her. No matter how many times he did that, it startled her every time. She jumped.

"Can I ask you a question?" Tally asked.

"As long as it's not the one women always ask men, 'Do I look fat in this dress?' Because even though I'm two hundred years old, I'm still too smart to answer that one."

Tally laughed. "No, it's not that. Who was the old woman in my mirror?"

"The woman who cursed me."

"Why is she so angry?"

"She's the grandmother of the woman I seduced and begot twins."

"Why is she mad at me?"

"I do not know. You will have to ask her."

"I don't particularly want to talk to her."

"I cannot fault you. She was the one who turned over your furniture."

"Really. Why?"

"She was trying to distract you from your beau…ah, lover."

"Did she cause the other interruptions? Is she haunting my sister, too?"

"No doubt."

"Well, she should relax because the lover's only temporary. You hear that, Grandmother? He's only temporary."

"Why do you say that? It seems like you enjoy his company."

"I like directing my own life. I only hired him to help me search for my brother and get the map back."

"Love doesn't force you to give up your independence, it changes to interdependence."

"Who said anything about love? I don't believe in love and fairy-tale endings. That bunk is for suckers."

"Is it? How about your neighbor Madame Alain. She and her husband were very happy here. I should know. I used to see them walking the court hand in hand, every day, until death did part them."

"Love isn't for me, Captain."

"I thought I told you to call me Gabriel."

"You did. Sorry. I went to a museum today to check it out and see if it would be a good place to set up your exhibition."

"That is capital."

"I haven't talked to the curator yet, but I'll do that soon. In fact, I'm going to start cataloging the contents of the attic on my day off—tomorrow."

"I will help in any way I can."

FINISHED FOR THE NIGHT, Tally exited her dressing room in the back of the Blue Note. She met Chuck, the owner, in the hallway.

"I wanted to talk to you before you left," he said.

"About what?" Tally asked.

"I've had a very good offer on the Note."

"Are you accepting it?"

"I'm afraid I'll need yours right away."

"Can you give me another two days, Chuck? Please. That would be just shy of the two weeks you promised me."

"I'll give you by close of business two days from now. I'm sorry that I can't wait any longer, my daughter needs me."

Tally stood in the hallway a few minutes longer, cursing her luck. This was all Mark's fault for being so juvenile and petty.

She felt sick inside thinking that he might have lost the piece of paper detailing the whereabouts of the captain's treasure. She loved her brother but he was letting her down without even knowing it. She had to find him.

She couldn't really depend on anyone, a lesson she'd learned over and over again.

Then she came out into the restaurant to find Christien waiting for her. Everything inside her went hot and she thought she was going to have to amend that statement. She could depend on Christien, but she didn't want to. It hurt too much to lose that support.

Breathtakingly gorgeous and sinfully sexy, he strolled over, brushing at the loose strands of his hair. Christien usually wore it back, but tonight the silky strands were loose around his face. The private greeting in his eyes started a slow sensation in the pit of her belly.

"Where you at, *chère?*" he murmured, his tone as warm and intimate as the genuine affection glimmering in his eyes.

Every nerve ending zinged as she responded to the delicious smell of him by breathing deeply. "Nowhere." The word slipped out sounding tortured even to her ears.

His smile faded and he studied her. "That doesn't sound good. What's wrong?"

The urge to tell him was so overpowering she had to clench her teeth to hold back. No. She couldn't let herself depend on him for anything except finding her brother. She would not let herself be sucked into a relationship that could cause her so much heartache. In her world, people, even the ones she loved, let her down. With anguish, she realized that was true. She depended on him and she hated the thought of it. Better she step back and keep all her secrets to herself.

"I've had a frustrating day, that's all."

Christien stared at her with those intelligent eyes of his that seemed to reach deep into her soul and tug on emotions she'd spent years keeping under wraps.

She grew uncomfortable beneath his penetrating gaze and wondered if he could sense her internal guilt—her duplicity.

She looked away and inhaled a deep, calming breath.

"I thought you said you trusted me?"

She winced at the guilt that roiled inside her. "I do. But I can take care of myself, Christien. What I need you to do is find my brother."

He backed her up out of the milling patrons into the hallway behind the stage.

"You know something, *chère,* I'm not doing this for the money or because it's my job. I'm doing this for you."

His palm cupped her jaw, warm and, damn him, but so reassuring. And his nearness, the length of his body pressed against hers in the dim hall all put a sensual spin on what was a comforting gesture. To distract herself from her emotions, she deliberately leaned forward and put her mouth on his. Her pulse fluttered in her throat as she vividly remembered the exquisite feel of those fingers stroking over her body, petting her. The way they'd slipped deep inside her sex and set her on fire.

Christien pulled away, staring deep into her eyes. "Is that your way of telling me to mind my own business?"

"I was kissing you, Christien."

"You were distracting me, *again.*"

"Please don't push me tonight," she pleaded, knowing that she was weak, so weak where this man was concerned. If he pushed, even a tiny bit, she was going to spill her guts and get in too deep. It was only going to make it harder for her to end it later. And end it she would.

"You tie me up in knots, Tally," he said pressing his forehead against hers.

And once again, he didn't let her down. He backed

off and gave her the space she needed to pull all those crazy needs and deep-seated emotions back.

"I've got some good news for you," he said.

"I can sure use some."

"I checked your brother's bank account too soon. He was still in town when you hired me. We must have missed him at his apartment."

Tally groaned. If only the timing had been right. "What did you find out?"

"He took five hundred dollars out of his account the day after you hired me. Nothing's changed about your brother's whereabouts. He's still AWOL," he went on unaware of her relief. "Other than what I've told you, I'm at a dead end with Mark. The rest of this case hinges on finding out what the band knows. Let's hope they can give us the information we're looking for."

She nodded, knowing he was right.

TALLY SAT AT A TABLE in a small hole in the wall on Bourbon Street. The revelers were out in force tonight getting a head start on the drinking. Christien was talking to the lead singer of the Calendar Boys, the band who supposedly knew where Mark could have gone.

She could see how they got their name. Every

single male, from the drummer to the lead singer, was drop-dead gorgeous.

Tally still couldn't believe that she didn't know anything about Mark's life outside of the family get-togethers. She made a mental note to rectify that as soon as they found him.

She took a drink of her club soda as she watched the two men talk. Then she saw the man Christien was talking to shake his head and something snapped in Tally.

She rose from the table so quickly, she almost tipped it over. Approaching the men, she could see that the lead singer's jaw was thrust out, his eyes spoiling for a fight.

"What's going on?" Tally asked, interjecting herself between the two men.

"He refuses to answer my questions."

Tally turned to the lead singer. "Look. What is the problem? I need to speak to my brother. I'm worried sick about him. If you know where he is, why won't you tell me?"

"Whoa," Christien said, taking Tally's arm and trying to pull her back.

The lead singer threw a sidelong glance to the drummer who shrugged his shoulders.

"Mark told me he was leaving town for something really important. He didn't tell me where he was going or when he'd be back. He said he wanted to surprise you and your sister."

"I can't wait. I must speak to my brother. It's urgent."

"I'm sorry. I don't know where he is."

"If you do speak to him, could you please let him know I need to talk to him?"

"I will."

Tally turned, knowing that they'd hit another dead end. She put her hand on Christien's chest. "Let's go."

They left the bar and walked to where Christien had parked his Jeep.

"Where to now?"

"Home, please. I'm exhausted."

"I just need to make a quick stop first if that's okay with you?"

"Sure, Christien."

Tally slumped in the seat as Christien drove, trying to work out in her head how she was going to get enough money together at this late date to buy the Blue Note, but she came up empty-handed. The Blue Note was the culmination of everything she'd planned for and now that was slipping through her fingers. Her heart squeezed hard in her chest and she blinked rapidly trying to push back the tears clogging her throat.

"Hey, we're not beat yet. I'll figure something out."

Tally closed her eyes tight against the pressure to cry, the tenderness in Christien's eyes hitting her harder than the thought of losing the Blue Note. His sweetness only made the tears press harder to the back of her eyes.

"Thank you," she managed to say.

Christien pulled up in front of a restaurant. "I just have to go inside for a few minutes. I'll be right back."

She watched his lean form disappear and thought stupidly that her world was falling apart and Christien was getting takeout?

The bizarre twists that her life had taken lately weighed her down. Captain Dampier's ghost, the grandmother ghost who Tally was sure wasn't done with her yet, Kachina's serious advice about her mother, and the loss of all her plans.

But when Christien came back out, a white paper bag in his hand, Tally couldn't help the leap her heart made. His face illuminated for a moment in the lamplight made her admire what a dangerously attractive man he was.

"What are you doing?" she asked.

He turned to her with a wicked gleam in his eye. "Got something to cheer you up."

"What is it?" she asked, reaching for the bag.

"Oh, no, you'll have to wait to find out."

She sat up straighter and tried to grab at the bag. Christien whisked it out of her way, grabbing her around the waist and setting her back in her seat.

He was like a little boy with a secret and her mood changed and lifted at the seductive grin he gave her.

His hands lingered at her waist and drifted up her sides. His mouth hovered over hers, but didn't descend, just tantalized. Her lips tingled in anticipation, but he kissed the corner of her mouth, pressing his jaw along hers.

He gathered her against him and just held her.

It felt too good.

Tremors radiated through her. She felt thoroughly possessed by him, body and soul, in a way that defied their impersonal bargain and the simplicity of an affair. In a way that aroused feelings that had no business being a part of this short-term relationship.

At the moment, she couldn't seem to care that she had to keep her distance. Wanting and needing were all that crossed her mind.

When he pulled away, she was glad to see the passion in his eyes, but something else warred in his hot brown depths. Before she could analyze that last emotion, before she could dwell on what she had seen, he pushed away from her and started the engine.

Tally settled into the seat. Only three days after she'd hired Christien, she was already losing her resolve to remain detached.

She remembered how she didn't want to get in too deep.

Too late.

10

As soon as Tally closed the door of her town house, Christien slipped his arms around her. His mouth, hot and open, caressed her lips and she lost herself in the sensual haze. He slipped his hand under her T-shirt, cupping her breast, another gripping her bottom through her pants.

Her curiosity got the better of her; gasping for breath, she placed a hand on his chest to hold him at bay. "What do you have in the bag?"

"You'll see."

Her gaze remained on his face; his stare sank deep into her heart. From the first, he'd possessed the power to see too much.

He went into her kitchen and grabbed a bowl out of the cupboard.

Looking up at her earnestly, he said, "Do you have candles upstairs in your room?"

"Yes, but—"

"No questions. Go on up and I'll be there in a minute."

"You can be very high-handed, Mr. Castille," she said, turning away.

"Yes, I can."

Up in her room, she lit the candles, three on the dresser and three each in her windows. Making her way over to the night table, she lit the two sitting there. When she turned to go around the bed to light the other two, she shrieked and jumped back. Captain Dampier stood right next to her.

Christien called from downstairs. "Are you all right?"

"Got too close to a candle," she called out and quickly closed the bedroom door. "Did you forget our ground rules?"

"I wanted to give you a warning. The crone is very angry. I really don't know that she can harm you, but I wanted to let you know."

"Thank you. Now get out of here."

He hesitated, looking more ghostly in the candles' glow. The hair on the back of her neck rose, the reality hitting her again. She was talking to a ghost.

"Did you find your brother? The map?"

"No. Are you sure you can't remember where it is?"

"I cannot recall. I am sorry," he said as he started to fade away.

There was something about his eyes that made her think he was lying, but why would he lie? There wasn't anything he could gain from it.

He disappeared just as Christien opened the bedroom door carrying a flaming bowl on a tray. The interior of the bedroom took on a warm glow.

"What is that?"

"Cherries Jubilee."

"That's one of my favorite desserts. How did you know?"

"It was an educated guess."

He set the tray on a nightstand and grabbed Tally's hands. "Come on."

She let him pull her toward the bed and Tally had an insight into Christien's behavior. He was offering her comfort. The comfort of food and sex. His comfort. She sat close against him and finally, for the first time, let herself lean on someone else.

He stroked her hair away from her face. "I won't let you down, Tally."

"Thank you," she said, his hand soothing against her skin. But she couldn't quite let go of her wariness. The most important person in her life had let her down so many times and most of her relationships since had been very unfulfilling.

Until Christien.

Turning her face away from the dessert's eerie blue glow, she faced Christien, his deep brown eyes welcoming, compassionate and sincere. Fear warred with the need to confide in him. She'd labeled him a heartbreaker before she ever knew what kind of man he was, but now that word took on a whole new meaning. He was so much more, yet the danger to her heart was very, very real.

She was afraid that she hadn't really grasped the true meaning of love. But love was fleeting. Everything in her life taught her that. The only constant was money, the ambition her key.

"I'm going to buy the Blue Note. It's the only thing that means anything to me."

He cupped her cheeks and feathered his thumbs along the hollows. His eyes taunted her with an awareness of exactly what she was trying to do. He wouldn't have any of the distance she hoped her words would evoke. That was all that was left of her defenses.

Christien breached them with a soft smile and even softer eyes. "I believe you could rule the world, Tally, if you put your mind to it."

She closed her eyes for a second as his mouth replaced his thumb, his lips soft against her skin.

The alcohol on the dessert was burning low, indicating it was almost ready to eat. Christien pulled her top over her head, his mouth going to the ridge of her collarbone. Her nipples puckered, his fingers working the clasp of her bra until it came undone and her breasts were freed.

Gently, he cupped her breast and sucked her nipple, pulling hard with his hot wet mouth.

Swallowing a whimper, she closed her eyes and gripped his shoulders. His tongue licked and swirled, and his teeth nipped, sending waves of heat rolling through her. Long, questing fingers grazed her belly.

He removed his mouth and Tally felt a warm sticky substance against her other breast. She looked down to find that Christien had smeared melting cherries over her nipple.

"Time for dessert," he said softly before his mouth covered the spot. He sucked and licked every bit of the concoction from her flesh.

She gasped as his parted lips worked the aching tip, bringing a rush of moisture spiraling to her core.

Christien backed off and stood, quickly ridding himself of all his clothes. His cock was hard and fully aroused. Completely, unabashedly nude and all hot and aroused for her, he stole her breath away.

Back on the bed, he reached for the button of her jeans and released it. Curling his fingers into the waistband, he pulled both denim and lace down her legs and off. Before she could move, he slipped his arms around her calves and dragged her toward his waiting mouth.

His finger dipped into the bowl of dessert and he drew a line all the way to the top of her sex.

His hot mouth went to her belly, sticky with the warm cherries. Each stroke was like sweet torture as he lapped at her, cleaning her with each swipe.

Once more his finger delved into the bowl, scooping out morsels of the dessert. Depositing the mixture onto her clit, his thumb stroked against the hood of her sex.

She gasped, her voice filled with excitement. "What are you doing?"

He looked at her with dark, daring eyes. "Seeing if I like all my cherries hot."

He dipped his head, his upper arms flexing as he leaned forward bracing his palms on her inner thighs to push them farther apart. With his thumbs, he gently pressed her open, revealing the heart of her pleasure to his hungry eyes.

He groaned soft and low, causing Tally's hips to lift from the bed in anticipation of that clever mouth and tongue around her sex.

She didn't have long to wait as his mouth covered her, his tongue tasting her with a long, slow lick. She caught her breath at the exquisite sensation, hovering between ecstasy and surrender.

His rough cheeks abraded her inner thighs adding to the tingling heat pulsing inside her clit. When his tongue dove inside her, Tally cried out, the trapped air in her lungs released in a whoosh of sound.

His mouth closed again over her pulsing clit, and his tongue circled it with twirling pivots, accelerating her heart rate until it was pounding like a bass drum. He took her fervently, hotly, voraciously, sending her over the finely honed edge of orgasm.

At that moment, she met his stare and she watched him take in every nuance of her pleasure. The look in his eyes was open and honest and, for the first time in her life she felt a connection, deep, abiding and strong. No promise was spoken between them and Tally was grateful for that because she wasn't sure if she could make any guarantees. The intensity was too much, as if she'd opened a box expecting to find nothing and instead found everything.

He slid up her body and pressed his palms against hers, lacing his fingers with hers. She tightened her grip, savoring the warmth in his touch. Suddenly, a calming sense of rightness settled over her. She knew that what he offered her, what she wanted from him, went deeper than just physical. Emotions were involved. How deep those emotions went, she didn't know. All she knew was what she needed.

Wanted.

More.

But she felt the resistance the moment she thought those words. A resistance that was like a big wall rising up and up.

Christien was everything she wanted.

But all that she feared.

He gave her no time to dwell on the images as he said, "Spread your legs for me."

As she parted her thighs to make room for him, he grabbed one of the condoms, tore open the package with his teeth and rolled the latex down his shaft. Sheer primal lust shimmered off him in his quick, efficient movements. She witnessed his hunger as he swept a heated look up the length of her.

A muscle in his cheek clenched in barely controlled restraint and his nostrils flared.

"Wrap your legs around me, Tally."

There was a warning in his tone broadcasting that his control wasn't going to last long.

Staring into her eyes, he pushed into her an inch, teasing them both with his hot shaft. "When I get inside…" he said, "I'm going to lose it." His voice was a rough growl.

"I want you, Christien, just you."

He slipped into her, strong and deep, and Tally accepted him all the way to the hilt, crying out in pleasure and realization.

His eyes flared wide in response, giving her a brief glimpse of passion, heat and something else warring in their hot brown depths. Before she could analyze that last emotion, before she could dwell on being consumed by him, he began to move, his body grinding against hers as he increased his pace.

A low, throaty moan escaped him, and he seared his mouth to hers, kissing her with a fierce passion that caught her off guard. His tongue swept into her mouth, matching the pistoning stroke of his hips and the slick penetrating slide of his flesh into hers.

Tremors radiated through her from the sensitive spot where they were joined so intimately. She felt thoroughly possessed by him, body and soul.

Pushing all thought aside, she concentrated on the pleasure he gave her, and how alive he made her body feel. Running her hands down the slope of his spine, she curved her fingers over his taut buttocks to pull him closer and abandoned herself to yet another orgasm.

This time, he was right there with her when she reached the peak of her climax. Groaning, he broke their kiss and tossed his head back, his hips driving hard, his body straining against hers.

"Tally." Her name spat out between his clenched teeth as his body convulsed with the force of his release.

When the shudders subsided, Christien lowered himself on top of her and buried his face against her throat. His ragged breathing was hot and moist against her skin, his heart racing as fast as her own.

A smile drifted across her lips as she trailed her fingers back up his spine, all the way to the damp, silky tendrils of hair at the nape of his neck, savoring the feel of him inside her, draped over her. She'd never felt so utterly satisfied, so sexually and physically content.

Though these feelings only stirred her deep-seated fear that she was clutching on to him for different reasons.

He turned onto his back, bringing her against his body and it wasn't long before his quiet, even breathing told her he was asleep.

CHRISTIEN WOKE HER in the night, his hard-muscled skin rasping against her cheeks. His mouth captured her nipple, his fingers already on her sex, rubbing at her clit until she was moaning in the darkness.

He spoke in rapid French, almost too fast for her to understand—concentrating on his words at that moment was beyond her. His wicked hands were stealing away her reason until she mindlessly moved against his fingers, the aching core of her tingling and pulsing with a desire only he could fulfill. She climaxed hard, her back arching with the intense pleasure of it.

Then he was inside her, her waning orgasm still throbbing with each thrust of his hard cock until he cried out and collapsed against her, rolling until they were entwined once again.

But this time Tally couldn't fall back to sleep. Cautious and quiet, she disengaged her legs from Christien's and slipped out of bed. It was barely five o'clock. More than anything, she wanted to stay in his arms. Wanted to make love with him again. She couldn't, she reminded herself.

Now that they were at an impasse in finding her brother, Tally was more restless than ever.

Still, she couldn't bring herself to leave him, not yet. She padded across the floor toward the bed. Christien lay on his side, one arm stretched out. Waning light coming through the window splayed across his square jaw and high cheekbone; his hair was rumpled from the fingers she'd tunneled through it.

Reaching out, she stroked a fingertip across the inky thickness while emotion tightened her throat. The hold he had on her heart was alternately comforting and terrifying, and she wondered where they would go from here.

She closed her eyes against the tightness that settled around her heart. She couldn't just stand there wondering about what the future held, not when th present pressed down on her with such urgency. She had made a pledge to herself to secure Gabriel's treasure and forge ahead with her plans. Later, she would examine her feelings for Christien. All she knew for sure was that they had created a powerful bond between them. A bond far different and more compelling than she'd felt with any other man.

A LOUD THUMP WOKE CHRISTIEN. He opened his eyes and at first was disoriented. Then memories came flooding back. He was in Tally's bed, in her room.

He smiled when he heard her muffled curse above him and had to wonder what had gotten her out of bed so early on her morning off.

He stretched and marveled at how good it felt to be here.

Staying in her bed all night long had felt amazingly, perfectly right.

Standing, he slipped on his underwear and jeans. He could smell the wonderful aroma of coffee. The plan: downstairs for a cup, then up to where it sounded like Tally was shoving around furniture.

In the hall, Christien tripped, feeling as if two

hands had settled like ice against his bare back and pushed. He smelled the scent of burned ashes, candle wax, and thought for a brief second he'd heard the sound of drums. His thoughts scattered as he fell forward, but caught himself just in time.

Resting for a moment against the polished wood as adrenaline surged into his system, he turned to look behind him and caught the sight of something. He blinked and looked again, but nothing was there.

Feeling a bit foolish, he descended the steps slowly.

Tally must have decided to move the boxes from the office up to the attic. He remembered she'd said something about sorting artifacts that had to do with the captain.

In the kitchen, he pulled a cup from the cupboard and went to the counter and poured coffee from the pot. He'd been content to date casually without commitments. Keeping his emotions out of the equation had been easy, but this morning realized that it was a matter of finding the right woman. Now, making promises was all he could think about.

His short time with Tally was no longer just about great sex and how compatible they were in bed. He was more aware than ever, that with each moment that passed, being her temporary lover wasn't going to do it for him. He wanted—needed—more than a short-term affair.

His focus had shifted and there was no going back. He wanted to move forward, get her to commit to him, have her voice that this feeling inside him wasn't one-sided.

On the way up the stairs, Christien could hear the sound of Tally's voice.

"Is the spyglass one of yours?"

As he reached the top of the stairs, he saw Tally standing in the middle of a ton of boxes, old clothes, maps and furniture. In one hand she held an old spyglass, the brass tarnished, and in the other, she held a rag.

"Tally?"

She whipped around and smiled in that strange way as if he'd caught her doing something she shouldn't.

"Hey, there's coffee downstairs."

"Already had a cup. Followed my nose. Can I help you out?" he asked.

"Sure. I was just about to polish this." She looked self-conscious and wary.

Her tone was reserved, too, as was her expression, which Christien found ironic since that should have been his reaction to their intimate morning-after situation.

"You didn't have to stay the night just for me, Christien."

Christien took the spyglass and rag out of her hands.

He found a place to sit and started polishing the eyepiece.

"Do you always talk out loud like that?"

"I didn't even realize that I was doing it. Did you get something to eat?"

"No, not yet. Maybe when we get some of this handled, we can go down to Café Eros and get one of Chloe's beignets?"

"That sounds heavenly. I've gotten a lot done."

"What time did you get up?"

"About five. After we made love, I couldn't sleep."

And he noticed she averted her eyes. He was quite sure it wasn't because of modesty. The fact that she'd left the bed in the wee hours of the morning the first time they'd made love wasn't lost on him.

"So do you usually spend the night?" she asked slanting him a speculative look.

"Not usually."

She blinked at him, obviously shocked by his confession. Then the significance of his comment sank in, and a quick flash of alarm shimmered in her eyes. Was he going too fast for her? At this point, he decided he had no choice, because he suspected he only had a handful of days left to convince her that they were meant to be together. He wanted her in his life. Permanently.

He loved her.

His heart pounded hard and fast. An adrenaline rush swept through him as he finally put the words to the emotions tumbling around in his chest. He didn't fight the sentiment, didn't deny its existence. Instead, he allowed it to flow through him, and let himself get used to the feeling of knowing that this one special woman complemented him so perfectly, in ways that made him feel whole and complete, physically and emotionally.

He kept his revelation to himself for the time being. He suspected that if she knew the depth of his feelings for her, she'd panic and withdraw from him more than she already had this morning. And that wasn't a chance he was willing to take with her and their relationship just yet.

He slipped his arm around her waist, lowered his mouth to hers and kissed her with a passion that seemed to grow stronger every time he touched her. Her hands came to rest on his chest, and his mouth seduced hers until she finally gave him what he wanted from her—a soft, surrendering sigh and the tension in her limbs replaced with the press of her lush curves against him.

"You're pretty good at that, Christien."

"Thanks."

"Lots of practice, I bet," she laughed lightly and

moved smoothly out of his embrace, still skittish with the morning-after intimacy.

He'd hoped to ease her misgivings about staying the night, but the glimpse of insecurity he detected in her tone spoke volumes. It also gave him another clue that she was feeling uncertain about the change in their relationship, and about him.

"Listen to me. I sound jealous. Sorry for the third degree." She backed up, knocking over a small box. The lid opened and the contents spilled out.

She looked around dismayed, but he took her hands in his, wanting to soothe her. There had been many women in his life, but Tally wasn't just another woman. Not any longer. He recognized and accepted that fact. And he supposed it was time he offered up a little proof to her of that realization.

He touched his fingers beneath her chin and raised her gaze to his. Her wide eyes flickered with a vulnerability that wreaked havoc with his insides. A vulnerability he took very seriously.

He drew a deep breath and tried to reassure her of his intent. "I've never told any woman the things I've told you, Tally. Ever."

She looked at him, her eyes searching his, and then she seemed to shut down, but moved into the circle of his arms. "You're a very sweet man," was all she said.

He held her for a few minutes, and then she broke away from him. "I'd better get everything sorted, now that I've made a start."

Christien bent down and began to put the contents of the small box back inside when he saw a white envelope with flowers all over the face. Tally's name was written in a beautiful feminine hand. When he turned it over, the envelope was sealed.

He realized it had never been opened.

He turned to her and held up the letter. "Tally…"

She saw the envelope and snatched it out of his hand. She threw it back in the box, quickly shoveling in everything else that had tipped onto the floor before Christien could make out what anything was.

"Tally, it hasn't been opened."

"I know," she said in a clipped tone.

"But…"

"I'm not going to open it, Christien."

"Why?"

"It's from my mother."

He wondered when, if ever, someone had been there for Tally or if it was in her nature to protect herself and keep her emotions locked up tight inside her. She was afraid of losing the people she loved and her coping mechanism was to stay distant. The arguments with her brother, her misplaced belief that she could shove her mother into a box and close the lid.

The emotions of that strong and important relationship just didn't die. He knew.

While Christien intended to give her brother a
dressing down for worrying his sister, Tally had to
face the fact that Mark was a grown man and could
lead his own life. He didn't condone the way that
he'd decided to treat his sister. It was clear he wasn't
going to kowtow to her anymore. It was clear in his
absence, his silence. And any resulting consequences
were Mark's to bear.

All Christien could do was show her that he'd be
there for her, to make sure she knew how much he
cared. In the meantime, he'd protect her to the best
of his ability and do his damnedest to locate her
brother and end her worry.

After that, any future they might have together
was up to Tally.

11

IT SEEMED THAT EVERYTHING about today was utterly disturbing. Having Christien fill her bed and her room with his unsettling, sexy presence, having him confess to her that she was very special to him, and now her memory box turning over, spilling out painful secrets she never wanted revealed to anyone.

Her hand trembled as she slammed the lid back on and shoved the box under a table.

The captain was still standing in the corner of the attic. He'd been telling her what was his and what wasn't while Christien had slumbered below her. Now he remained there, his eyes filled with compassion and a gentleness that she thought would have been beyond a two-hundred-year-old ghost.

"Do you want to talk about it?" Christien asked, his voice soft.

"About what?"

"About that box and the letter."

"It's simple. My mother left and she wrote me a

note. Big deal. Do you think that anything she has to say will make me hate her less? I had to give up everything to care for Mark. It was her responsibility, not mine. And now, I can't even get Mark to find something worthwhile in his life. Here he is running around doing a menial job when he has so much talent inside him."

Christien tried to step toward her and soothe her, but Tally sidled backward.

"I need you to find my brother. Everything I want hinges on him. Don't ask me for details. Just, please find my brother."

"I promised you I would. I won't let you down and I would never ask for something you're not willing to give."

"I'm getting desperate, Christien. My time is running out."

"Maybe if you would really trust me…"

"I trust you to find my brother."

She knew if he touched her she would lose this edge she'd developed. She needed that edge to keep her away from that box under the table, the same box that was locked and buried deep in her heart.

"You love your brother and you want the best for him."

Love. There was that word she was trying to avoid. The single word made her yearn to embrace all the subtle changes in Christien she'd noticed the past few days. Those qualities were becoming increasingly difficult to ignore or dismiss with a pat excuse. There was no denying the tenderness and genuine affection in his gaze when he looked at her, as he was doing now. Nor the way he touched her that had nothing to do with sex and everything to do with an understanding she'd been without for too long.

Love. An emotion she'd thought was an illusion—and was rapidly being disabused of that notion. It was everything Chloe had said it would be: wonderful, yet so complicated and scary for all it implied.

She exhaled a shaky breath and refocused on the next box. "Can we drop this, Christien? I really need to go through this stuff."

He nodded and she was grateful that he didn't push her. She was on the verge of a total meltdown.

He picked up the spyglass and began to polish. Tally fell into an easy routine of holding up objects for the captain to see and pass judgment on.

It was late morning when Tally called a halt. Christien lead the way from the attic to the second-storey landing. He stopped to brush dust off his jeans. Tally passed him. "I'm going to take a quick—" The word *shower* turned into a shriek as Tally felt two ice-cold hands propel her forward. The dizzying fall down the stairs rushed up at her.

Two strong, warm arms snapped around her middle and pulled her away from the dangerous fall as she and Christien crashed to the floor, both gasping for breath.

"Are you all right?"

"I'm fine, thanks to you. You always seem to be there when I need you."

As the words tumbled from her mouth, her heart opened a little bit more to let him in. She was losing her battle to stay distant from this man as she let herself sink into his arms.

"WHAT THE DEUCE DO YOU THINK you are doing, crone?" Gabriel said to the old woman at the foot of the stairs.

"Trying to separate them."

"By hurting Tally or, worse, killing her?"

She turned shadowed eyes on him. "It wasn't her I was trying to push, you fool! It was the man."

"You are trying to injure a living being."

"He's a threat to her."

"I will not stand for this, crone. Be warned that I will not let you harm the man."

She gathered her shawl around herself and gave him a haughty look. "Do not pretend you are noble, Gabriel. It doesn't become you." She disappeared.

Gabriel watched as Christien gathered Tally

close to him and their auras blended more beautifully and harmoniously than they had been in the café. It was happening and there was nothing the crone could do to stop it. They were falling for each other.

But Gabriel had seen how Tally had acted in the attic toward Christien. She was afraid. And he realized what the crone had wrought when she'd blessed her descendants with ambition. She'd taken from them their courage. The courage to take a risk on what Gabriel had learned too late.

Love.

She'd robbed each and every one of them.

Tally and Christien stood up. Gabriel studied the tender way Christien pushed her hair out of her face and he was struck with a deep dilemma. Convincing Tally to embrace her love for Christien wasn't going to be enough. She had to want it with her heart and soul. Yes, she was falling for him, but wasn't yet at a place where she could accept what he had to offer.

That damn curse. In that moment, he knew that he couldn't do what he'd set out to do. After getting to know Tally, he, quite literally, loved her like a daughter for her generosity in trying to elevate him to a place he'd wanted to be many centuries ago. If he'd had a heart still beating in his chest, it would be aching right now.

Tally was on the verge of the most powerful love of her life and she was too afraid to reach out and take it.

There would never be another man who would even come close.

And for her, for Christien, he mourned.

Gabriel waited downstairs until Tally was alone and Christien had left the house. He appeared to her as she came down the stairs.

"I told you that old woman doesn't like me very much—she tried to push me down the stairs."

"She does not like me either," Gabriel said in commiseration. "But it's Christien she was trying to hurt. You just got in the way."

"She doesn't want me to be with Christien?" Tally's eyes widened. "She'd better not try that again," Tally said through gritted teeth. "Leave him alone."

Gabriel resisted the urge to sway her thinking. Now that they had formed this bond between them, more was at stake than the breaking of the curse. Tally's heart was engaged, but her head was keeping her back. "What do you want?"

"Mark safe and the treasure found so that I can buy the Blue Note."

"And where does your man fit into your life?"

"He doesn't."

"Then, why fight the crone? Just tell her what she wants to hear."

"No one tells me what I can and can't do."

"Ah, the courage of your ancestors does rest in you."

"Courage. What is courage, really?"

"It's going into battle against great odds without hope of winning."

"Why did you do it? You owed New Orleans nothing, especially since they treated you so poorly, before and after."

"New Orleans is my home and no foreign army was going to take that away from me, not while my heart beat in my body."

"So exposing yourself to something you would normally avoid is courage?" Tally asked.

"Courage is facing risks, whether it's facing down the British Army or facing your own doubts."

"So, courage is having the guts to stand up against what you're afraid of and realize that it is worth fighting for?"

"Ah, I truly wish that I had spoken to you sooner, young woman. But things happen in their own time."

Tally nodded. "I'm off to get you a wing of the museum, Gabriel."

He put his hand to his heart and bowed. "I'm honored by this gift you are giving me, Tally."

TALLY LEFT HER TOWN HOUSE with the conversation swirling in her head. She was a person with a logical, practical mind. If a thing made sense, had a reason behind it, she could understand it at least. But things that struck from out of the blue defied logic. There was no reason, no explanation she might find some comfort in. That left her with nothing, nothing to cling to, not even hope, because in a world where anything might happen at any time, unpredictability shoved aside and left fear in its place.

That was why the treasure was so important to her. Money was tangible and would give her the security she needed in an insecure world.

It was all she would need.

When she got to the museum, she was ushered into the curator's office.

Jennifer Sutton was blond and petite. She smiled at Tally. "What can I do for you today, Miss Addison?"

"I would like to speak to you about setting up a wing of this museum for Captain Gabriel Dampier."

"Captain Dampier was rumored to be part of the rebellion that saved New Orleans. Pity that we don't have any tangible proof."

Tally wasn't about to admit defeat. She would have to convince this woman that Dampier deserved a place.

"I have his journal and collected a large number of his possessions."

"A journal is promising and would document his contributions, but it would be so much better if we had something more. Corroboration would be ideal. Lafitte's contribution is not only word of mouth or through his journal. There is much to prove he played a vital role in the defense of the city."

"No, not anything concrete. But I feel that he should be honored as one of the men who helped save New Orleans."

"Keep looking and I'll see about space in the museum. When could I come by to view the artifacts?"

"I've got a little bit more work to do. I'll get in touch with you as soon as I'm ready."

"It's all very exciting, isn't it? Dampier is well known as a pirate. Why, he built the 'hot' court near the French Quarter."

"I live there."

"How lovely. We don't take these matters lightly. Please bring me the journal when you can and keep trying to find corroboration. Of course, for a man who lived in the eighteenth century, we would be very interested to see what artifacts you have that could serve as an exhibition."

Tally realized that she wasn't going to get any farther with this woman and fumed as she stood to shake her hand. "I'll get you your proof, Miss Sutton. You can be sure. I'll be in touch."

CHRISTIEN WENT TO HIS OFFICE and started writing up a report each for two clients. Trying to find Mark Addison, tailing his robbery suspect and spending time with Tally had put him behind.

After working for a couple hours, he was interrupted as Tally slammed into his office.

She sat down in his chair with an irritated sigh.

"What's wrong?"

"I went to the museum today to talk about introducing Gabriel."

"You say his name like you know him."

Tally stared at him, startled by his statement. "What?"

"It's as if he's a friend of yours, not some two-hundred-year-old ghost."

She met his direct gaze, an unreadable look in her eyes. "I guess I feel, after all this time spent with his artifacts, that I do know him."

"What happened at the museum?"

"The curator told me that although it's been rumored that Gabriel had played a large role in the protection of New Orleans, there was no concrete evidence that the story was true."

"So where does that leave you?"

"The curator said she would be happy to look at what I had and she could possibly set up a display for him, but they couldn't help me with his contribution to history. He would just be a figure that once lived in New Orleans."

"That's something, isn't it, Tally?"

"No," she said, erupting from her chair. "It isn't. He was an important contributor and I want him to receive the accolades he deserves."

"Then you'll have to find something concrete to prove that he played a hand in the protection of New Orleans."

She smiled and it touched him profoundly. "You're right. Getting angry and railing about this isn't going to get me anywhere."

His cell phone rang and Christien flipped it open when he recognized Jim's number.

"What's up?" Christien said into the phone's receiver.

"Chris, I need your help. I've got a hot case I'm working on right now, but I don't want to stop keeping tabs on the suspect."

"Jim, I'm busy right now."

"Look, Christien. He's jumpy and I'm worried he's going to break today. The signs say so, but I've got to follow this lead before it gets cold. I'm asking for an hour of your time."

"Jim…"

"He could kill another woman today. Do you want that on your conscience?"

"I'm not on the force anymore." But the guilt constricted his chest. Maybe he could do this one last thing. Maybe he could get some form of justice for the slain victims and their family members.

"If you weren't so stubborn… Christien, just an hour, buddy."

"An hour. Where do you want to meet?"

Jim gave him the location and Christien snapped his phone shut.

"Who was that?"

"Jim Carter."

"Is this about that suspect you've been following?"

"Yes. Jim needs about an hour."

"Could you give me a lift back to the court? This day isn't turning out like I planned. It seems that nothing is turning out like I planned."

"You know what they say about best-laid plans, Tally. Besides, just because she turned you down doesn't mean you can't do anything about it."

Once in the car, Tally asked, "So this guy is pretty important to you?"

"He was. I've stopped pretending that I'm still on the force. I left and I should start paying attention to my business." Those words and the meaning behind them left a hollow pit in his stomach.

"Just because you left the force, doesn't mean you can't go back any time you want."

Christien exhaled heavily. "The system sucks."

Her expression grim, her eyes dark from emotion, she said, "But it's what you've got to work with. Isn't that better than not doing what you love?"

Christien gripped the wheel, her words making too much sense to him. "I've made up my mind."

"You don't sound happy about it."

"I am being realistic. There's usually no happiness in that."

Before she left the car, she touched his arm. "Christien, this may not be any of my business, but I think you can't forgive yourself for letting your mother down. Every time you lose a case, it only makes it worse. Maybe what you really need to do is let yourself off the hook. Accept that there will be some you win and some you lose."

He clenched his teeth against the swell of emo-tion; the guilt pressed down on him. "I don't like to lose."

He could feel her watching him, judging his response, waiting for more.

He took her hand off his arm and brought her across the seat with a quick tug. His mouth met hers briefly before he let her go.

"Are you willing to give up the chance to win because you do lose once in a while?"

"I've got to go."

She nodded and got out of the car. Christien drove over to the suspect's place of business and traded off with Jim, receiving a wave from him as he drove away.

Minutes later, the suspect came out of the garage and got into his car. Christien started his Jeep and gave it a few minutes before he pulled away from the curb. As he drove, Tally's words floated through Christien's head. Keeping his eye on the blue car, Christien noticed when they entered the Garden District and anticipation roiled inside him when the suspect parked on a side street, one block away from the cased victim's house.

The suspect sat in his car for a few minutes, edgily looking around. Christien parked far enough away to belay any of the suspect's suspicions, but close enough that he could keep the guy in view. Christien heard a knock on his window just as the suspect opened his car door. Opening the window, he smiled at an old man.

"You lost, mister?"

"No, but thanks."

The old man looked skeptical, but left the vehicle. The suspect was already on foot, disappearing down the street.

Christien reached for his glove box and took out his gun. He almost reached for a radio to call for backup, but remembered that he wasn't on the force anymore. He was on his own.

He slipped out of the Jeep. The old man continued to water his lawn and darted glances Christien's way. Tucking the gun into the small of his back, he took off after the suspect. Deliberately staying far enough away so as not to spook the suspect, Christien trailed him. If he made him, Christien might lose his chance to catch this guy red-handed.

The suspect got away from him momentarily, so that Christien had to run to catch up. Then the guy disappeared into some undergrowth. Christien skirted the growth and climbed a fence. Dropping down into a backyard, he came face to teeth with a huge black Doberman.

The dog growled. Christien turned and made for the fence. But just as he was going over, the dog got a hold of his leg and bit down hard, breaking the skin. He lashed out and the dog let go. Christien jumped over the fence and landed on the ground hard.

When he rolled, he winced as he put pressure on his leg, but he ignored the pain and skirted the fence, judging it was safe to go the same way as the suspect. When Christien reached the white clapboard house, he saw a broken window.

Without hesitation, he climbed through. Bringing his gun up in a two-handed grip, he moved silently through the bedroom until he reached the living room.

"Tell me where the money is and I'll let you live."

He had a woman by the hair and was pointing a gun at her face. Silently, Christien moved into the room. The woman saw him and her eyes widened. The attacker whirled.

"Detective Castille. What a nice surprise. Drop the gun or I'll blow her head off."

Christien really had no choice. He started to lower the gun, then the old woman balled up her fist and hit the suspect right in the groin as hard as she could.

The suspect howled and swore, but immediately collapsed, letting go of her hair. Christien motioned her over to him.

The woman didn't hesitate. She ran over. "Thank you so much," she said.

"Call the police. Quickly!" Christien ordered.

The suspect, breathing hard, looked up at him.

"Brought down by an old woman. Now that's poetic justice," Christien said.

"So, what do you get me for now, huh? You couldn't get me for those murders. In fact, you'll never get me for them."

Just like he would never get justice for his mother.

The gun in Christien's hand trembled. All he had to do was pull the trigger and this man would never put another life in jeopardy.

"What are you going to do? Shoot me? You don't have the stones, Castille."

Christien's fingers tightened, all the guilt and frustration of twenty years manifesting itself in this one moment. He took in a breath and held it. Then he heard Tally's voice. *Do you really want to give up winning because you lose every once in a while?* How could he look into her eyes if he pulled the trigger? How could he look into his own?

He relaxed his hand on the gun, but kept it trained on the suspect, only relinquishing his vigilance once he was cuffed and taken away.

AT THE PRECINCT, Christien finished writing up his account of the incident. As he put the pen down, his captain approached the desk. In his hand, he had both Christien's badge and his department-issued gun.

"When are you going to take these back, Castille?"

"How about now, Captain?"

"Yeah, now's good."

"The department let you hold on to these for a year?"

"Yeah, since I put in that you had taken a leave of absence. Welcome back, Castille."

After the captain was gone, Jim slapped Christien on the back. "You did it, man. We got that guy dead to rights."

Letting out a breath he hadn't realized he'd been holding, Christien smiled broadly. "Yeah, we did."

With those words, he was finally able to let the past rest, let his mother rest and forgive a six-year-old boy who had failed to get the justice his mother so richly deserved. He would do what he could and work within the system. He'd learned the hard way that it did mean something.

His calf throbbed. One of the paramedics who had arrived on the scene on the heels of the police had bandaged him up and given him a tetanus shot.

When his cell phone rang, Christien answered for the last time. "Castille Private Investigations."

"Mr. Castille, this is Bobby Green. I'm the drummer for Calendar Boys."

"Right, we met last night."

"I got your number off the card you gave to our lead singer. I don't know where Mark is, but I can tell you he has a girlfriend. Her name is Marie Lamarouex."

"Do you have a number for her or know where she lives?"

"No. That's all I know."

"Thanks for the information."

"Hey, I don't know Mark that well, and he's one hell of a musician and songwriter, but he doesn't know jack about how to treat his sister. I have one, too. I wouldn't want to see the worry on my sister's face that was on his sister's last night. Not cool, man."

Christien turned to the computer and accessed the information he needed on Marie Lamarouex.

He tried her number, but there was no answer. He left a message for her to call him back. Deciding to take a ride over to her apartment, he rose.

He'd finish up this job for Tally, then he was going to tell her how much he loved her, that in his darkest hour, she'd been the one who'd shone through to save him from committing an act that would have haunted him for the rest of his life.

A life he wanted to share with Tally.

_12_

DISCOURAGED, HOT AND SWEATY, Tally sat down on a box and wiped the sweat off her forehead. "Are you sure there isn't anything here that proves you helped Lafitte?"

She addressed Captain Dampier who, by the way, didn't look hot and sweaty. He looked transparent as usual.

"No, I don't think so. I detailed some of the planned strategy in the journal."

Tally shook her head. "I've already read that over. It's not enough. She wants something concrete, not an account from a man who once had a reputation as a notorious pirate."

"I am not a pirate."

"Sorry. I'm just repeating what she said."

"Narrow-minded individuals. Even two hundred years later, I cannot get my due."

"You'll get it. I promise you that I'll keep looking."

Tally's cell phone rang. Her heart stilled in her chest and she lunged for the ringing phone.

"Hello, Mark?"

"No, I'm sorry. This is Marie. Marie Lamarouex. I'm Mark's girlfriend."

"Do you know where Mark is?"

"Yes, as a matter of fact, he's at his apartment right now. He just got back."

Tally was already rushing down the attic stairs. "Thank you very much."

"Mr. Castille was here and he told me what you've gone through. That was really irresponsible of Mark. I wish I'd known sooner."

"Thanks for phoning," Tally said and ended the call in her haste to get to her brother. Jumping in her car, she sped over to his apartment, smiling with relief. She took the stairs two at a time until she reached his door. She knocked.

When her brother pulled open the door, all the frustration and anger seemed to well up in her and detonate into a ball of fury.

"Where have you been?"

His mouth thinned into a straight, mutinous line. "I had to do something. Something important."

Releasing her pent-up breath in a rush, a lump formed in her throat. "And you couldn't have called me?"

He stared at her, swallowed and looked away. "I was mad at you. I came over to your place to tell you good news and you start in. You always start in."

Looking at his handsome face, thinking about all that she had been through with him, the emotion simmered inside her, the lump in her throat thickening. "I'm not having this argument with you right now, Mark. Do you have any idea what you've put Bree and me through?" Covering her face with her hand, she started to cry, the emotion too intense to hold in. A wave of relief swept through her that her brother was all right and he had come back. She was so happy that he had come back.

His voice full of regret, he awkwardly hugged her. "Don't cry. I'm sorry, okay?"

Tally hugged him back. "Call her as soon as I leave so that she knows you're fine and please don't do this again."

"I promise I won't. Marie told me I was being selfish and juvenile and she was totally right."

"She sounds nice. I hope I get to meet her soon." Now that she was assured he was okay and she was sure he wouldn't pull such a stupid stunt again, her mind shifted. "Mark, you took something from the house the day you left. You ripped a piece of paper out of an old journal."

"A piece of paper?"

Tally felt her insides turn to ice. "Yes, from an old journal I left on the counter."

"Yeah, that was the oddest thing. I was looking for paper and then I heard a riffling of pages and there was this blank one."

"Mark, do you have it?" She clutched at his arm.

"Somewhere, I'm sure, but I can't quite remember."

She collapsed against the door frame. "Please, Mark, you've got to find it for me. It's vital."

"What is it?" Mark asked.

Tally was dimly aware that she was digging her fingernails into her palm. "It's Captain Dampier's treasure map."

Mark started to smile, but then must have seen the irrefutable panic in her eyes. "No kidding?"

"I've actually talked to his ghost."

"Uncle Guidry said there was a ghost, and you've talked to him? While sober?"

"Yes." She rolled her eyes. "I wouldn't lie to you. I've been looking everywhere for you, so I could get the map back. There's really a treasure and I want to use the money to buy the Blue Note. I even hired a private detective."

"I know." Mark opened the door and Tally's heart sank as she saw Christien standing in her brother's living room. His eyes were very cold.

"I used the map to take down directions and I know I still have the scrap of paper somewhere."

"Directions?" she asked. "To where?" Tally's eyes never left Christien.

"I wanted to wait until you and Bree were together, but, since you've ruined everything anyway, I might as well tell you."

"Tell me what?"

"I'm going to the Berklee College of Music in Boston. That's where I was, auditioning."

"What?"

"I've saved everything I've made for the last eighteen months."

"Please tell me you're not doing this because I nagged you into it. I want you to do what you want to do, Mark. Not what I want you to do."

"After all the nagging and all the lectures, you're actually trying to talk me out of this?"

"I just want you to find your own way and I promise that I'll stop nagging you. I just wanted the very best for you, that's all."

"This is what I want to do."

"Bree and I can help pay…."

"No, I wanted something that's my own, Tally. You've provided for me since Mom left. Don't you think I know what you had to give up for me? Don't you think that bothers me? You and Bree have had to take these mundane jobs because of me. I wanted to spare you having to pay my college tuition, too. But it seems that I didn't have to worry. I got a full scholarship."

"Oh my God. I'm so happy for you. Why couldn't you just have told us?"

"I wanted it to be a surprise."

Christien walked toward the door, brushing past her as he left.

"Christien."

He watched her with an intensity that made her heart climb up her throat and nearly stall. Finally, he hauled in a deep, uneven breath, his eyes fierce with emotion. "You could have told me, Tally," he whispered huskily.

"I couldn't," she replied, her voice quiet. If she had trusted in him that much, leaned on him that much, and he had let her down, she would never have forgiven herself for being such a weak fool. Love was an illusion, after all.

"Why?"

Tally looked away. The silence stretched out between them, and she shifted her feet, trying to blink away the burning sensation in her eyes. "Because it's not about us, Christien."

He folded his arms across his chest. "No, you made that clear a few moments ago. I was just your P.I."

She met his stormy gaze head-on. "I told you I had plans," she said. She shook her head and looked away. "They're more important than anything."

"Your plan to buy the Blue Note?"

She nodded.

He snorted. "This isn't about your plans. This is about your fears. You're afraid to love me. You need security, and love gives you no guarantees, but real estate and money do."

When she didn't answer, he gave her a humorless smile. "Did you think that I would try to undermine your plans?"

She answered immediately, "No." Her voice soft and uneven. "I told you that I don't need a hero."

"So you did. Glad you got what you wanted." He stalked away.

Mark sighed. "Looks like you're batting a thousand, sis."

Tally drove home on autopilot. She tried not to think about Christien. As soon as she walked in the door, the captain appeared and she couldn't seem to show any reaction.

"Did you get the map?" he asked, his eyes taking in her face, a face she tried to keep neutral. When his eyes filled with sympathy, she knew she'd failed.

"No."

"What happened?"

"Christien didn't know about you or the map. I deliberately kept it from him. I didn't want anyone else involved."

"Would he have believed you?"

"I think he would have. He feels betrayed." She rubbed at a headache behind her eyes. "By me."

"He has a right to. Does your brother still have the map?"

She turned dazed eyes on him. "I think so. He says he can find it."

"What are you going to do about Christien?"

"I don't know. Tell me what you think I should do."

She studied his ghostly face and his kind eyes, hoping for some kind of answer.

"You have to do what is best for you, Tally."

Her shoulders slumped. "I'm going back up to the attic to search for something to convince the museum curator that you are an authentic rescuer of New Orleans. Are you coming?"

"In a minute," Gabriel replied as he watched as Tally walked listlessly up the stairs. He might be a ghost dead for two hundred years, but his heart was breaking for her right now.

"You could have told her what she wanted to hear," the crone said in a soft voice.

"I know."

"You can't break the curse without her."

"I know!" Gabriel said, turning on her. "Leave me be, old woman. I'm not willing to manipulate her for my own gains. She has to make the decision for herself."

The crone's eyes narrowed. "What kind of trick is this, Gabriel?"

"It's no trick."

"You would not give up this opportunity to break the curse. I know how much you want eternal peace."

"Because you want it, too, Belle."

"Don't call me by my first name," she said and disappeared.

"Are you coming?" Tally yelled from the attic.

HOURS LATER, STILL SWEATY, hot and disappointed, so disappointed in the outcome of the day, Tally went into her bathroom and started running the water.

She'd never forget that cold, hurt look in Christien's eyes as long as she lived. Suddenly weary, she couldn't even seem to dredge up enough worry whether or not Mark could find the map.

She'd lost something precious today and it had nothing to do with buried treasure.

She sat listlessly on the edge of the tub and swirled her hand in the water.

"You are better off without him."

Tally's head jerked up toward the mirror to find the old woman staring at her.

"There can be no place for love in ambition, girl."

Calmly, Tally picked up a round candle on the side of the tub and threw it at the ruined mirror. It hit with a satisfying splintering sound.

THE DAY AFTER CHRISTIEN had closed Tally's case, he sat at his desk. He had already contacted his landlord and terminated the lease. He was heading back to the force tomorrow, but his enthusiasm was dimmed.

He wished he could have stayed angry at Tally. Somehow that would have been easier than this ache in his heart that wouldn't go away. But Tally was too caught up in her own fears. Fears he understood. She had decided to give up any chance at a future with him.

Releasing a heavy sigh, he packed the last of his files in a box near his desk. His phone had already been disconnected and he just had to return the keys to the landlord on his way home.

"You closing up shop?"

Her soft voice startled him so much, he dropped the files and they scattered across the floor. He glanced up at her as she came forward and knelt down to help him.

An odd sense of déjà vu washed over him. It had

been just over a week ago that she'd shown up in his office asking him to help find her brother, starting an affair that had changed his life and turned out to be more than he'd bargained for.

When they both reached for the same file and his hand brushed hers, she jerked back. He had hoped she'd come here to tell him that she wanted to continue their relationship or what he most hoped for. That she loved him.

But by pulling away from him, she told him that wasn't the case. He stacked the files haphazardly into the box and rose, setting the box on his empty desk.

"What can I do for you?"

"First, tell me what's going on here? Are you no longer a P.I.?"

"Yeah, I'm a cop again."

"That's wonderful."

He smiled in spite of himself.

She smiled in return, though the motion didn't completely ease the guarded look that was back in her eyes, a tangible sign for him to keep his hands to himself. So he did, no matter how much he ached to reach out and touch her, to pull her into his arms. And hold her.

"How did that happen?"

"You were right all along, Tally. I'd rather lose some than not have a chance to win at all."

"And the suspect you were tailing?"

"Caught him red-handed."

"Why were you limping? Did he hurt you?"

"No. I went over a fence in pursuit of the suspect and got a very unhappy Doberman who had no problem letting me know it."

She winced. Her eyes flowed down his body and back up again. He clenched his teeth at the longing he saw in her gaze.

"So, why are you here?"

She fidgeted with her keys and her tone was distant, evidence that she hadn't come here to resume their relationship. She was all business, as if they'd never been intimate.

"I just wanted to thank you for everything you've done for me, and for finding Mark. I'm so relieved that he's okay."

"We found Mark together," he pointed out, doing his best to keep a tight rein on his frustration.

"Regardless, I appreciate your advice and guidance along the way."

She tucked a strand of hair behind her ear and shifted on her feet. "You know that Mark can't find the map, so I guess it serves me right for worrying about it at all."

"I'm sorry about that, Tally. I'm sure it means a lot to you."

Her chin came up at his hard tone. "I brought you this." She extended a plain white envelope. He could see how the paper trembled in her hand.

He sat down in his desk chair, making no attempt to take what she offered him. "What's in it?" he asked even though he knew what was inside the sealed envelope.

She thrust the envelope at him. "You know what it is. It's the rest of the money I owe you for finding Mark. Don't be difficult. Just please take it."

His mouth hardened and a tiny muscle pulsed in his jaw. He knew what he wanted to tell her and it was too important for him to blurt out in anger. Dangerously important. But he didn't want to push her. He knew a stone wall when he hit one. He'd had more than he could take of her need for independence. Her blatant need to throw his help right back in his face. He resented the fact that with the check she offered, she thought that ended their relationship, tied it up in a nice little bow.

"Is that all that's between us? A transaction?" He stared into her beautiful, fearful brown eyes. "I told you at the Blue Note that this wasn't a job for me. This relationship might have started on business, but I'm not ending it that way, Tally."

What he wanted, she wasn't willing to give and he couldn't take it or make her go against her fear.

She blinked rapidly, not willing to give an inch, ruled by deep insecurities that controlled too much of her life.

She stiffened defensively. "Don't do this, Christien. It's hard enough, don't make it worse."

"How could it get worse, Tally? Does what we shared mean anything to you?" he said, unable to hold back the roughness in his tone. "When are you going to stop hiding behind treasure maps and real estate?"

"I have no idea what you're talking about," she said, her denial coming much too quickly.

"I believe you do." He rose and she stepped back, her hand with the envelope dropping to her side. He didn't want his words to cause her pain, but he really didn't have anything left to lose.

"It's easier and safer for you to have plans and stay independent. If you don't let another person in your life, you don't risk getting hurt. I don't want to hurt you, Tally—I want to love you. But you have to let me in."

She shook her head jerkily. "I wish it was that easy," she said, her voice husky and loaded with regret. "I've got to stick to my plan and that doesn't involve anyone else."

He held up his hand, bringing her excuses to a halt. "Are your plans *so* rigid that you can't fit anything else into them? Did your mother leave only yesterday? Don't let your baggage rule you, *chère*, handle it and then together we can move forward."

Reaching out, he ran the back of his fingers down her cheek, the skin so silky and soft. "You need to take risks, otherwise you'll have nothing but things around you. Life is about living fully and, without love, how can you do that? Don't let that day come when you wake up all alone with nothing but regret for what might have been. Grab it now with both hands. Let me be there for you to lean on, support you, hold you."

Her silence broke his heart. "Give me that chance," he whispered. "Give *us* that chance."

Looking away, she let out a shaky sigh.

Taking her hand and turning it over, he pressed a kiss to the center of her palm. Her fingers trembled against his jaw, and he knew he'd said everything he could.

The rest was up to her.

"I'll be here, Tally, waiting. You know I'm not very good at that, but I'll try, for you."

She set the envelope on his desk and glanced at him one last time before she turned and left.

The tears in her eyes shredded him, hoping that this wasn't the last time he would see her, hoping that she would find the courage finally to give her heart to him without fear.

TALLY SAT ON ONE of the park benches in the piazza, bundled in her jacket, while a sharp wind blew across Court du Chaud. The miserable feeling wouldn't leave her whether she was waitressing, surrounded by customers at Café Eros, or singing at the Blue Note.

She'd kept her mind and hands busy the entire day in an attempt to work off the uneasy feeling that had plagued her since she'd walked out of Christien's office the previous afternoon.

She watched people move about the court, curling her hands around a cup of Café Eros's strongest brew.

Idle since she'd gotten home from work, she had too much time to think. Too much time to replay her conversation with Christien in her mind. Too much time to question herself, her actions, her life and her future.

Too much time to wonder if letting Christien go and believing that was for the best was about the stupidest notion she'd ever had.

He loved her.

The mere thought made her chest tighten and her pulse race. The last night he'd made love to her had been magical, a joining of not only their bodies but their hearts as well. She might not have been able to speak the words aloud, but there was no denying that she'd fallen in love with him, too.

She just didn't know what to do about it, because her fear of letting Christien in her heart was stronger than her desire to let him so completely into her life.

Sighing discontentedly, she dragged her fingers through her hair and took another drink of her coffee. The warmth settled inside her and took away the bone-deep chill. Unfortunately, there was no remedy for the ache in her chest.

Besides the loss of Christien, Mark hadn't been able to locate the map. She'd missed the deadline for the Blue Note and she was sure that Chuck would sell the restaurant to the person he had waiting in the wings.

She set down her coffee and eyed the memory box she'd brought down from the attic and placed on the bench beside her. It was time for her to open it and face her fears.

She opened the dusty lid. Six years ago, she'd returned from college and had begun to care for her brother. At that time, she'd put a bunch of things from childhood and her college days into this box along with the flowered envelope from her mother.

Bitter and angry, she'd had no intention of opening the envelope to read her mother's excuses. Tally had only hate for her.

The first thing in the box was a photo of Tally standing between two women she'd met in college, women she was sure would have turned out to be great friends.

She felt the loss of not only her chance to pursue her plan of becoming a businesswoman, but the relationships that never came to fruition. The loss of those experiences the result of her abandonment by her mother.

The second piece of paper was her first-semester class schedule, the classes she'd had to withdraw from. She set it aside after taking a moment to remember her thirst for learning and the sheer pleasure of each moment spent in the classroom.

She went through the box, noting every memory, soaking up those past times until she came to a picture of herself, Bree and Mark all sitting in their family room right before Bree and Tally had been scheduled to start college. Tally had her nose in a book, Bree was sewing a dress for her prom and Mark was strumming a guitar.

She'd had so many plans then, so much ambition.

Finally, she picked up the envelope from her mother and broke the seal. She pulled the letter out and opened the stiff pages.

Dear Tally—

I haven't been the best mother to you. I fear that it is best if I leave. Hand Mark over to you for safekeeping as I would fail him as I have failed both you and your sister. I will say what I have to say to you. Although you probably won't listen to me now, maybe one day it will all be clear to you.

Don't fall into the same trap that I've fallen into with searching for something that's empty. I've lost love and time with my frantic search for wealth. The old adage is true. It can't buy you love. Make your brother and sister understand.

The only real thing in this life is love and the people you share that love with. Please don't forget me.

Love, Mom.

The words were a balm to Tally's heart. The hatred she'd harbored, the resentment and the pain all dissolved to leave her feeling wrung dry.

Suddenly there was someone standing in front of her.

"Found it!" Mark exclaimed, handing the map to her.

Tally threw her arms around him and hugged him close.

"Wow, the thing means a lot to you."

"It's not the map, Mark. I've been so terrible to you. Pushed you to succeed, denigrated what you love to do. I'm so sorry about that. I don't think I've ever told you how much I love you."

Her brother blushed and shuffled his feet. "Ah, sis, I've always known that. Stop getting all mushy."

Tally brushed at her eyes. "Aren't you staying?"

"Nope, I've got a date with Marie."

"You don't care about the treasure?"

"I care, Tally, but not more than I care about Marie. Let us know if you find it. See ya."

She leaned back and looked at the sky, her heart squeezing so tight in her chest. What had she done? Christien had been nothing short of wonderful to her and she'd thrown everything right into his face.

The captain's voice penetrated her misery. "Tally, I see that your brother found the map."

"Yes, he did." She held the folded paper in her hand.

"Then let's look at it and go find the treasure."

She nodded. But made no move to unfurl the map.

Tears pricked at the back of her eyes. The captain looked at her expectantly.

"Something wrong?"

"No, I can't do this right now."

"What do you want to do?"

Tally sprinted to the door of her town house, opened it and sped to the phone.

13

CHRISTIEN WAS JUST FINISHING up his shift when the police captain called from his office.

"Castille, get over to number one Court du Chaud."

Christien came alert. He recognized the number of Tally's town house immediately.

"What's up, Cap?"

"There's been a robbery."

Christien used his siren to get over to Tally's town house as fast as he could. He took the stairs two at a time and opened the door as soon as he heard her say, "Come in."

He entered the foyer and saw her standing at her kitchen counter.

"What happened?"

"Someone stole my heart."

His body responded to that provocative voice, even while he wondered what she was up to.

"Who?" he asked, playing along.

"You."

"Is that so? When I heard about a robbery here, I guessed someone might have stolen your important map."

"This map?" She held it up. "I learned that some things are so much more important than money." With those words, she set the map into a bowl and, with the lighter she used for candles, set it on fire.

"Tally!" Christien jumped forward, but it was too late, the old paper had already burned to ash.

There was a sudden ringing tone that settled throughout the house. And he realized what she was saying.

She came around the counter and wrapped her arms around his neck. "The map doesn't mean as much to me as you do."

What had changed and why? He intended to find out.

Ever since she'd walked out of his office yesterday, he'd been distracted, his mind constantly thinking of Tally and wondering if he'd pushed her too hard and fast for a commitment. Wondering if he'd lost her for good because he wanted and needed her love like he needed nothing else in his life.

And now here she was, taking the first step to contact him when he'd believed it was over between the two of them.

He wrapped his arms around her waist, pulling her

closer to him. "What about the Blue Note and your plans?"

"You mean my wonderful dreams? I'll continue to save my money and hope that another lucrative property comes along that I can buy."

"Tally, what are you saying?"

"I made a terrible mistake." Regret infused her soft voice. "I was wrong not to embrace your love, so very wrong. I'm sorry if I caused you any pain."

"It's all gone now." A slow smile curved the corners of Christien's mouth and he ran his hand through her loose hair.

"I'm so glad," she breathed, smiling with eyes full of passion and, dare he hope, love.

"Circumstances might have brought us together, and this affair has been more than I ever could have expected, but when I'm with you, I feel like I've finally found the other half to my soul."

Christien's hand stilled in her hair. His heart beating fast in his chest.

"I knew I had to trust my feelings for you," she said, a vulnerable catch to her voice.

He pressed his forehead to hers. "And now?"

"I'm ready to take a chance on you. On us."

"That's no sucker bet," he said. Adrenaline and elation pumped through Christien. "What changed your mind, Tally?"

"I opened my mother's letter and through her words, through my own soul-searching, I found the courage to forgive her for leaving me, for all the things she's done in my life that have made me so fearful, because it's also made me the person I am today and I'm proud of the woman I've become."

That revelation pleased him; it was high time she recognized what he already knew. *"Ampère-heure, chère, bon pour vous."*

"It is good for me. You're good for me," she said, her brown eyes shining with hope and affection and confidence.

She held his gaze, her expression glowing with the kind of promises he longed for with this woman. "I love and trust you, Christien Castille. With my heart and soul, all of me."

She led him upstairs to her bedroom.

They came together in a deep, heartrending kiss. When he finally lifted his head, they were both breathing hard and he couldn't wait to get inside of her, be a part of her. He removed his shirt and then stripped off hers as well. She wasn't wearing a bra and he cupped her breasts in his hands, caressed her nipples with the brush of his fingers over the hard tips.

Closing her eyes, Tally sighed blissfully and arched into his touch. "I'm so sorry for what I put you through."

"It was all worth it. I love you, Tally. I want to be everything for you. I'm so happy that you let me in. I'll be there for you. I promise."

"I'll be there for you, too." She wrapped her arms around his neck and brought his mouth to hers in a silent confirmation of their need for each other. He laid her back on the bed and their kisses grew more passionate, more insistent and impatient as they fumbled with their clothing, until they were both naked and unbearably aroused.

He moved over her, settling between her thighs, feeling her hot and wet against his shaft. So ready for him. But he didn't enter her, not just yet. For the moment, it was enough just to have her beneath him, the tip of his erection sliding against her lush sex.

She pressed a hand to his jaw and smiled tenderly at him. "Move in here with me, Christien. Stay with me always."

Growing serious, he finally slid into her, a perfect fit, and gave her yet another promise to believe in. "I will. Truth be told, with you here, Court du Chaud feels like home to me."

GABRIEL DAMPIER STOOD in the kitchen looking down at the map Tally had burned and still couldn't believe it. She'd chosen love over ambition. Stated it out loud. Said she loved Christien.

He was halfway there; he felt just a bit lighter, a bit more insubstantial.

"You've succeeded without even trying, Gabriel. Half the curse has been broken. Now you'll be turning your interest to Bree."

"Let me celebrate in this triumph first, crone. Besides, as I told you, I gave up trying to coerce her into falling for the private eye."

"You manipulated her brother into taking the map. You whispered in her ear that she should confide in the man. I'd say you did your share."

"She also collected my artifacts, argued with a museum curator, and tried to get me my rightful place in history. These things I never asked for, yet she has done them."

"She's a strong and deserving descendant," the woman acknowledged.

"She is worthy of the treasure."

"It's a shame she'll never be able to claim it."

Gabriel didn't answer.

THE NEXT MORNING, Tally pulled Christien out of bed to cook for her. "Come on, I'm starving."

Down in the kitchen, he started one of his favorite Cajun breakfast dishes. A Cajun cereal made with cornmeal. "*Coche-coche* is popular around my house. You'll need to practice eating it."

"Why? Will there be a test later?"

"As a matter of fact there will. My papère will be very impressed if you can eat it without choking. Anyone who has ever eaten *coche-coche* more than several times has gotten a little down the wrong pipe."

"I'm looking forward to visiting your family."

"All in good time, *chère*."

After it was cooked, he poured milk on it and set it in front of her. Taking a bite, she said, "Yum."

Christien saw something out of the corner of his eye. When he turned his head, a man stood between Tally's living room and her kitchen.

"Who the hell…?"

Tally's head snapped around and she choked.

"Do you see him?" Christien asked her.

"Yes, I do."

"Don't tell me…."

"Captain Gabriel Dampier. Christien Castille."

Christien swallowed hard when the captain inclined his head.

After a moment, the vision started to fade in and out. The captain stepped forward. "I don't know what's happening, but it looks like I'm out of time. Tally, the treasure is under the piazza."

"What?"

"My treasure, all of it, is under the piazza. I built

it myself with my own hands and I buried all my treasure underneath."

"Oh my God! I thought you couldn't remember."

He gave her a cryptic smile. "Enjoy it, my sweet girl and remember me."

"I'll never forget you."

And he was gone.

IT TOOK TALLY WEEKS to get permission from the New Orleans historical society to dismantle the piazza with the strict understanding that every stone would be replaced exactly as it had been built. In between that time, she'd talked to Chuck at the Blue Note and had found out that the buyer who had wanted the club had pulled out. Chuck said if she wanted the Blue Note, it was hers.

Now she had the permission in her hand to take apart the piazza. The press had gotten wind of the possibility of Tally finding Dampier's horde and they were out in force, surrounding the piazza with cameras bristling.

It took hours to clear away a fourth of the rock and as the captain had said, his treasure lay before her for the taking. Cameras whirred and a great murmur went up amongst the onlookers. With trembling fingers, Christien standing stoically at her side, Tally used the key she'd found to open the chest. Tally lifted the lid. A starburst of golden light stabbed Tally's eyes as the metal caught the sun. There was a collective gasp, but tears pricked Tally's eyes. It wasn't the doubloons she saw, it was the strategic plans haphazardly placed over the gold that was the real treasure.

She reached down and picked them up. There in Gabriel's sprawling handwriting were his notations and signature, and below that were Jean Lafitte's name and signature.

Tally turned and threw her arms around Christien. "I've got proof," she cried. "I've got it."

Two nights later, Tally, Christien and all their friends and family were packed into the Note. She'd persuaded Christien's father to cook for her and their guests and to make the temporary position a permanent one.

Later, after all were sated with food, Chloe came up to Tally and nudged her shoulder. "Told ya so."

"Still being a smarty-pants, Matthews?"

"In my nature."

"Looks like the Court du Chaud love bug has bitten me after all."

"I don't think that little devil is done yet," Chloe said. "So, is it everything I said it would be?" Chloe bumped her shoulder again.

"More," Tally agreed, looking at Christien with love filling her soul. "So very much more."

"Looks like you've gotten everything you dreamed of."

"Dreams. They're wonderful things." She had gotten her due way beyond her expectations. Mark was going to a wonderful college to study music, she'd arranged for a wing in the museum for the captain and set up a society in his name to help anyone who wanted to attend college.

The treasure she'd found had totaled in the millions, but it wasn't the cold hard cash she'd cared about. Helping other people realize their dreams was now Tally's focus. She'd been so blessed with the Blue Note, a place to celebrate food and music with tourists and New Orleanians alike.

Christien's suspect had been convicted of the attempted robbery, but evidence had been discovered against him in a rash of robberies in Baton Rouge and he was going to stand trial there.

She'd talked to a pirate ghost, battled with a grandmother ghost, found a hidden treasure, forgiven her mother and in the process set her own heart free to love and be loved.

Then there was Christien. Beautiful, wicked, tender Christien. All she would ever need or want in a man.

"Now all we have to do is get Bree hooked up," Chloe said.

Tally searched for her sister and found her talking to Christien across the room. She could only hope that her sister would find the kind of happiness Tally now enjoyed.

But that would be her choice and her journey. Tally realized that the captain had had something to do with pushing her and Christien together by having Mark take half the map. She had to wonder if the captain had something in mind for Bree, too.

Her thoughts were interrupted by the sound of an accordion. Christien's father stood up on the stage playing a Cajun dance tune. Soon Mark was at the piano banging out the rhythm and everyone got to their feet and danced.

Christien found her then, his dark eyes filled with the passion and love they both shared in their hearts.

He took her hand and pulled her onto the dance floor and she laughed so hard, tears rolled down her face when her brother started playing the Jerry Lee Lewis song, "Great Balls of Fire," using his feet to play the piano and belting out the words.

When Mark finished his rendition and took his bows to a clapping, laughing crowd, he stood up and started clapping, too, calling out Tally's name.

Tally took the stage of her very own place, rich in much more than currency. She met Christien's eyes as he sat comfortably sprawled at one of the tables.

The band started up and Tally sang to him, her eyes never leaving his. She sang of fever and longing, her voice thick with it. She had the experience to go by.

In the years to come, that fever would never dim as long as she had Christien by her side.

When the song ended, Christien walked up to the stage and took a black box out of his pocket. Getting down on one knee, he captured her eyes and in front of everyone said, "Tally, will you marry me?"

"Yes," she said simply as everyone clapped. Courage, she thought, was facing your fear and knowing what was worth it.

He slipped the ring on her finger.

This was so very worth it.

Thank you, Gabriel, she said silently and thought she heard his deep voice reply, *You're welcome.* She looked into her future husband's face and whispered as she embraced him, "Christien, I love you."

Epilogue

CAPTAIN GABRIEL DAMPIER WALKED across the courtyard, his step much lighter as he made his way to Café Eros.

He turned to look at the twins who had emerged from their respective town homes, Tallis and Breanne Addison. He watched them walk toward the café.

Just recently, he'd had the opportunity to view both their auras, which were lifeless pewter-gray, a gray heralding the sad fact that true love had never touched their beautiful souls.

Now Tally walked and talked with animation, her aura a gorgeous blue shot through with red. A woman with happiness and passion in her soul. A woman who loved and was loved in return by the simple act of forgiveness.

In her ability to offer that forgiveness, she'd given him part of his redemption. His eyes shifted toward Bree, her aura still dull pewter-gray.

It was time for him to turn his attention her way. It was time for Breanne to find her own love. It was time for him to go to his eternal peace.

All he had to discover was who would be the right man for her. This man would have to be strong to handle one of the Addison twins, strong in character, mind and body. Nothing less would do for one of his descendants.

But he had no worries. Bree would choose her own man.

And he'd just give her a little push into love.

ANNABELLE GUINEVERE DUBOIS also stood and watched the twins move across the court. Her heart softened when she saw the look on Tally's face. These women who so reminded her of her beautiful Madeleine. Perhaps she could find it in her heart to forgive the pirate for what he'd done.

"No," she said, her voice hardening. "I'll not go all maudlin because one of my precious descendants has been foolish enough to fall in love."

She focused on Bree. Gabriel wouldn't be free until Bree found her true love.

She intended for that never to happen.

No matter what it took.

* * * * *

Look for the next Red Letter Night story coming from Alison Kent, Going Down Easy *available January 2006!*

eHARLEQUIN.com

The Ultimate Destination for Women's Fiction

The eHarlequin.com online community is *the* place to share opinions, thoughts and feelings!

- Joining the community is easy, fun and **FREE!**

- Connect with **other romance fans** on our message boards.

- Meet your **favorite authors** without leaving home!

- **Share opinions** on books, movies, celebrities…and *more!*

Here's what our members say:

"I love the friendly and helpful atmosphere filled with support and humor."
—Texanna (eHarlequin.com member)

"Is this the place for me, or what? There is nothing I love more than 'talking' books, especially with fellow readers who are reading the same ones I am."
—Jo Ann (eHarlequin.com member)

Join today by visiting www.eHarlequin.com!

INTCOMM04R

If you loved
The Da Vinci Code,
Harlequin Blaze brings you
a continuity with just as many
twists and turns and,
of course, more unexpected
and red-hot romance.

**Get ready for The White Star continuity
coming January 2006.**

This modern-day hunt is like no other....

If you enjoyed what you just read,
then we've got an offer you can't resist!

Take 2 bestselling
love stories FREE!

Plus get a FREE surprise gift!